A *Man* IN

WINTER

"A Man in Winter by Katie Marie is a horror story on more than one level, weaving murder in with the tragedy of loss of oneself through dementia. My heart broke for Arthur as his mind took him away from the world, leaving him vulnerable and confused and desperate for justice for his beloved wife, Molly. Treating the subject matter sensitively, this writer has created a tale whose horror lies in its very real possibility."
—Stephanie Ellis, author of *Bottled* and *The Five Turns of the Wheel*

Is there such a thing as tenderhearted horror? Well, there is now. Katie Marie's ghost story, *A Man in Winter*, connected with me on such an emotional level. In my opinion, the world of fiction needs more stories told from the POV of the elderly, and Katie Marie certainly delivers on that score.
—Catherine McCarthy, author of *Immortelle* and *Mists and Megaliths*

A mesmerizing psychological mystery from an author who brings a refreshing new voice to horror. This is a quick read, but one that keeps the reader thoroughly intrigued and entertained from beginning to end.
—Catherine Cavendish, author of *In Darkness, Shadows Breathe* and *Dark Observation* (coming in September 2022)

A *MAN* IN WINTER

By Katie Marie

A Man in Winter
Copyright 2022 © Katie Marie

Edited by Elle Turpitt.
Proofread by Heather Cain

Cover illustration and design by David Román (Max Stark).
www.pictorem.com/gallery/Max.Stark
www.instagram.com/max_stark8/

First Edition: July 2022

ISBN (paperback): 978-1-957537-05-4
ISBN (Kindle ebook): 978-1-957537-04-7
Library of Congress Control Number: 2022936060

BRIGIDS GATE PRESS
Bucyrus, Kansas
www.brigidsgatepress.com

Printed in the United States of America

To all of those, who like Arthur, may one day forget us. We won't forget you.

Content warnings are provided on the last page of this book.

Acknowledgments

Thank you to my mum, who not only read to me when I was small (and did all the voices), but who was also my first ever reader; your encouragement and passion has kept me working.

Thank you to my Paul, for long conversations, thoughtful suggestions, and for making my life better in myriad ways.

Chapter One

We pulled up outside the cottage and even from the road you could see it was a hollow shell. The windows were curtainless and dirty, the faded paint was peeling on the frames. It wasn't the home it had been. Sophie helped me out of the car and let me walk up the garden path alone.

The garden was still neat; it had been my domain, and I kept it right. The boys had worked on it after I had moved out, to keep it nice for the sale. The grass was a healthy green, even and well fed, not a single weed breached the surface. The front door creaked as it opened directly into the living room. It was bare, colour changes on the brown walls showed where the units had been, flat spots on the carpet exposed where the couch had squatted.

"They're good kids." I looked around the empty cottage. "They mean well." I ran my fingertips over the fireplace, pointedly ignoring the dust; Molly had always been the one to dust. I had remembered to do it once or twice in the last two years, but the cottage had never looked the same after she died.

I walked through the living room, touching fixtures here and there. I stopped to look at the spot where the sofa had sat, visible now through the different shade in the carpet. I remembered the kerfuffle we'd had getting the new sofa brought in. Damn thing was far too big, Mike and I had tried for ages to get it in through the front door, the back door, we'd even tried one of the downstairs windows before we'd given up. Sophie had gotten that sofa while Molly and I purchased another more modest one. Then we'd bickered for days about where it would sit best, she got her way in the end, I always caved in to Molly.

I went through to the dining room into the kitchen and stopped. The little kitchen looked so much bigger without all our stuff clogging the worktops. This had been Molly's domain, the hub from which she led our small family. The downstairs loo was a testament to Molly's love of pink, while the upstairs bathroom had been a testament to my failings as a plumber. The spare bedroom, which was really just a junk room, had taken Sophie days to clear, the local charity shops had no doubt benefited from that. Molly had liked to hoard things. But she'd always known what she had and exactly where it was.

Lastly, I came to our bedroom. Sophie and Mike had replaced the carpets. The old one couldn't be saved after the night Molly died. Her blood had soaked deep, and I had been able to smell it. I could still smell it now. Even though the boys had torn the carpet up and put a new one down, Molly's blood was engrained in the floorboards.

Sophie sniffed and wiped her eyes when I came out of the cottage and closed the front door behind me for the last time.

"You done?" she asked. I nodded. We got back into the car and drove away.

"Thank you," I said after we'd left the cottage behind. Sophie sniffed again.

"This is the right thing," she said after a moment. "Those stairs were getting too much, and now you're much closer to us."

"You act like I lived in another country."

"I can't imagine you living anywhere but England, no other country would have you." Sophie took a deep breath. "It's not like you're leaving her behind. Mum wasn't a house." Her voice was shaking. I reached over and put my hand over hers where it rested on the gear stick.

"Sophie, your mum's in here." I touched my chest where my heart was. "And here." I tapped my forehead. "She's not in bricks and wood; she's in us." Sophie nodded and sniffed again. "But I will miss the cottage. It was a wonderful home."

"You know," she said after a moment of silence. "If this doesn't work out, or if you're not keen on the place or the people or anything else, you can move in with us permanently. Mike has almost finished the extension, so we'll have plenty of room. You won't have to stay in the guest room anymore. You'd have your space, your own shower. We could even put in a little kitchenette if you liked. It would be your own place, just attached to mine."

"And have me lose my marbles in front of your boys?" I scoffed.

"Don't say it like that," Sophie glared at me before turning back to the road. "Lots of people live really well with…your illness."

"Dementia, sweetheart." I swallowed the lump in my throat, she couldn't even say it. "At least living here if I forget to turn off my own oven then I'm only going to burn down my house, not yours."

"Dad!" Sophie snapped.

"I'm kidding," I said. "Thank you, love. I will keep the offer in mind. But let's give the old codgers a try before I relent and submit myself to the role of full-time grumpy granddad."

"You're not that grumpy," Sophie said, turning the car into the Willow Hill Retirement Community. The uniform bungalows that lined the narrow roads looked lived in and cosy. Net curtains lined the windows, which were mostly hidden behind hanging baskets and bushes. Small lawns squatted in front of the bungalows, all well mown and simple, some covered in gnomes, others bird feeders, and one was covered in plastic cats. Sophie pulled up outside a bungalow that was the same as all the others and smiled at me. "This is it."

"I'm going to need some paint," I said. Sophie raised an eyebrow at me. "The colour doesn't matter, but bright would be good. If not paint, then maybe a flag with my name on."

"Why?" she asked.

"How else am I going to know which one mine is?" I said.

Sophie laughed and got out of the car, coming around to help me as I struggled to get out.

"I'm sure we'll think of something. How about a rhododendron? Mum loved those."

"She might have loved them, but I didn't, damn things are awful." I smiled to let her know I was joking.

"How about a little greenhouse, then?" she asked as we walked up the short path.

"Oh! Are you a gardener?" a voice called. I glanced over at the bungalow on my left and spotted a short lady, dwarfed by a large grey overcoat. "My Gerald was good with his veg."

"Dad's a dab hand at carrots," Sophie said, leaning over the little fence to offer a hand to my neighbour. "I'm Sophie."

"Hello, dear." The lady smiled. "I'm Doris." She looked at me. "You're the new boy, then? I spotted your son-in-law here early this morning."

"Mike and I have been unpacking since six this morning," Sophie said.

"You are a good lot then," Doris said, turning away. "I'll let you get settled in. But don't hesitate to come over soon, you hear me?"

Sophie led the way inside. "She seemed nice."

"Busybody." I shrugged before looking around. The living room was all unpacked; Mike and Sophie had been very busy. They'd arranged the furniture the same as it had been at the cottage.

"Well," was all I could say.

The walls were chocolate brown on the bottom half, a lighter cream coffee colour on the top. The room was warm; the colours making even my old tattered furniture and battered ornaments look comfortable and inviting. This alien place was already feeling more like home.

"We put things where we thought you'd like them." Mike came in from a hallway on the other side of the living room. He looked even bigger than usual in the small room. Mike was Sophie's gentle giant of a husband. The man wouldn't have looked out of place chopping lumber, burly and bearded as he was, but he was more at home in the kitchen delighting his children by making intricately decorated cakes. "But if you want anything moved, just say."

"It's lovely, your mother would have adored it," I swallowed a lump in my throat.

"But do you?" Sophie put a hand on my shoulder. "You're the one who has to live here."

"It's grand dear," I said. "Very classic. Makes me feel like I should get a pipe and one of those red velvet house coats."

"Come on." Sophie tugged at me. "You've got to see the kitchen. It's so cute." She tugged again, and for a split second, I had a vision of her when she was five years old dragging me onto the playground or to see something interesting she'd found in the garden.

The kitchen was small, but it had what it needed. The units were in a horse-shoe around three of the walls, with the doorway taking up most of the fourth wall. The sink sat beneath a wide window and to the right of the fridge, which stood next to the doorway. If someone opened the fridge, they'd be blocking the doorway. Handy then that I was on my own.

"I tried to put things away logically," Sophie said. "The cups are in the cupboard above the kettle, the food is in the cupboards opposite to the fridge, cleaning stuff is under the sink."

"It's a small kitchen love," I opened the cupboard above the kettle and wondered why I had so many cups. "I'm sure I'll find my way around."

All the cupboards were white and looked the same as each other. Sophie and Mike had painted the small amount of wall space a light sea blue to complement the white cabinets and black worktops. It was bright, clean, and functional. The only thing I wasn't keen on was the long red strings, like the light switches you get in bathrooms. I'd seen the like in hospitals before, or disabled bathrooms; they were there to call for help.

"They're for if you have a fall." Mike stood in the doorway and caught me glaring.

"I've never had a fall in my life," I said. Mike looked at me with an eyebrow raised. "Ok, I've not had a fall since they put in the new hip."

"What about the wobble in town last week?"

"It was a wobble, not a fall."

"They come as the standard, Dad," Sophie came in behind Mike. "They're in all the rooms. Just ignore them unless you need them."

"Who comes when I pull one? The Justice League? Wonder Woman would be nice."

"Wardens." Mike rolled his eyes at me. "The main office is in the community centre, up where the hall is."

"Hall?" I remembered the kids mentioning a hall when they'd told me about this place. "Where the bar is?"

"Yes, Dad." Sophie sighed. "Where the bar is."

"Might give it a look at some point. Speaking of the bar, where is—"

"Your super-secret drink collection?" Mike said. I nodded. "The globe is in the living room, next to the sofa."

"Your mum and I brought that back from Italy." I walked over to the globe in the living room. It was beautiful, dark wood with gold hinges on the equator, allowing the globe to open up. The inside was hollow with a flat base a little way down which acted as a shelf for bottles.

"Yes, you brought it back because of its magnificent Italian craftsmanship, not because it's a drink cabinet."

"It was your mother's idea." It had been one of Molly's best thoughts. She didn't like a cabinet being used for drinks, and this was apparently a conversation starter. I liked it because it meant the whisky was close to the couch.

"Alright," Sophie said. "The bedroom's through there. I sorted it all out for you, the bathrooms next to the bedroom." She glanced at her watch. "I've got to go collect the kids, but I'll come round soon to make sure everything's alright."

"Ok." I nodded.

"The hall's good for more than a bar." Mike followed Sophie out. "There's a little cinema, a communal games room and a restaurant as well, so if you don't fancy cooking tonight, you don't have to."

"Thank you."

"You've got my number if you need anything," Sophie called from behind Mike.

"I've been perfectly alright for the last seventy years. I think I can handle this. Don't worry so much."

"Alright." Both of them held up their hands in a surrender gesture her mother had always done.

"I'll see you tomorrow, Dad. I'll drive you to your appointment." Sophie climbed into her car.

I watched both cars disappear around the corner.

With the cars gone, I noticed a young man in a uniform standing across the street, watching me. I assumed he must work here because of the uniform and raised a hand in greeting. A look of surprise crossed his face, and he slowed down to stare at me, frowning. I half expected him to stop and question me as to what I was doing, but he kept moving, watching me intently as he walked away. "What an odd boy." I turned back to head into the bungalow. "Might as well have a cup of tea, then." I patted my pocket for the flask I knew would be sitting there.

I made it to the kitchen before the doorbell rang. I sighed and turned back; tea would have to wait. Doris stood on the doorstep, a Tupperware box in her big knuckled hands.

"I'm sorry." She was a short lady, solidly built and stocky. Her hair was pure white and cut short. She had smile lines around her eyes and her breath smelt faintly of brandy. "I'm dreadfully embarrassed, but I didn't catch your name earlier."

"It's Arthur," I offered her my hand. "You're Doris." She took my hand and looked at me hopefully. I relented quickly. "I was just going to put the kettle on."

"Oh, thank you." Doris followed me into the kitchen. She put the Tupperware down and took off the lid. The smell of ginger wafted out. I looked at her.

"I met your son-in-law this morning; he said you liked gingerbread."

"Very kind of you." I opened cupboard after cupboard, looking for cups. Where had Sophie said she put them?

"Let me help." Together, we found where Sophie had put the cups, above the kettle, and the plates, in a lower cupboard close to the fridge. It took a bit of time, but we eventually found where she had hidden the tea bags as well.

"Sugar?"

Doris shook her head, examining the small plate in her swollen-knuckled hand. "These are beautiful."

"Molly picked them; she was always good at that sort of thing."

Doris put some of the gingerbread on the plate. "My Gerald, God rest his soul, didn't bother himself about things like dishes. He wouldn't have noticed if I'd have put his dinner on the cat as long as the beast was still."

I put the tea on a tray stand, a little thing on wheels, bloody useful. Sophie had got it when my hip went a few years back. I wheeled the tea and gingerbread through to the living room and sat down with Doris.

"So, your son-in-law tells me you're a widower?" Doris sat on the end of the sofa while I sat in the old armchair.

I nodded. "A little over a year since my Molly was taken."

"Gerald passed away two years ago. He said he'd wait until I went, he didn't want to leave me alone, but you can't help when you go." She sipped her tea. "It was cancer, in the end. I told him the cigarettes would do him in; he used to laugh at me." She looked at me for a moment. "It's nice to have a friendly neighbour again. Mr. Hamilton, the gentleman who lived here before you, he wasn't much for talking to a silly girl like me."

"Well, more fool him." I leaned over and reached into my pocket and pulled out my flask. It was an 8-ounce stainless steel flask wrapped in burgundy leather. Molly had bought it for me years ago.

"Would you mind?" Doris held out her cup. I smiled and topped her tea up. "Thank you. Gerald always laughed at me for nagging him about his smoking but then having a tipple to warm me up."

"Nothing wrong with a drink now and then."

"You'll be a fan of my cakes then," Doris laughed. "My son says there's more brandy than flour in them."

"I imagine I will be then." I took a piece of gingerbread. It was firm with a tad too much ginger, but not bad at all.

Doris explained she had lived here for three years. She had moved in three summers ago with her husband Gerald, who the old girl obviously missed more than she tried to let on. She ran the hall's bingo night every other Thursday and had two sons who visited when they could. Doris talked until the clock chimed seven and my stomach growled.

"Oh, I am sorry. I've been talking your ear off for far too long."

"Nonsense." I stood up, my back and knees stiff from sitting. "It's been lovely."

"Well, Maximillion will want his tea. Max is my cat, and he's none too shy about letting me know I'm late with his dinner."

"I didn't know they allowed pets here?"

"Oh, yes." Doris opened the door. "Well, it's been a pleasure, Arthur. Don't be a stranger."

"Nor you." I watched her walk down my path and up her own. "Good night, Doris."

"Good night, Arthur."

I closed the door.

"Pets, well, that is a pleasant surprise." I headed to the bathroom to use the toilet. I opened the door and laughed out loud. The bathroom was bright pink.

When I was done, I went into the kitchen and heated some of the soup Sophie had sneaked into the fridge during the move. "Maybe I'll get a little dog? Some company and a good reason to go out and about."

I was still muttering to myself about getting a little dog, maybe a Jack Russell, when I sat down in the living room and made a start on the soup. It wasn't bad; Sophie hadn't inherited her mother's skill in the kitchen, but she wasn't completely without talent. Molly had always teased us both that we could burn water, but Sophie had married well; her husband, Mike, was a chef at a local restaurant, so her skill never mattered much. I wondered briefly why Mike had let Sophie make the soup.

With dinner done, I flicked through the local news on the telly. I was watching a report on the tension in the Middle East when I must have drifted off.

I woke with a start to the sound of Molly calling my name. I blinked blearily around the living room, confused for a moment. The newscaster was long gone. I flicked the telly off and stood up.

I shambled past the kitchen, glancing in at the washing up. Resolving to do it in the morning, I headed to bed.

*****

"Arthur, wake up," Molly's voice was a hiss in the darkness. "Arthur, wake up, someone's in the house!" I rolled over and wrapped an arm around her.

"It's just the cat. Go back to sleep," I mumbled, pulling her close to me. She was warm and smelled like the fruity shampoo and rose-scented bath soap she used. Her normally soft body was tense in my grip and I could feel her trembling. I opened my eyes and looked at her in the gloom.

"Arthur, it's not the cat." There was a loud thump from downstairs. Someone was in the house. My heart instantly sped up, forcing me to take a few deep breaths to calm myself. Trying to remember my Air Force days and the tricks I knew for staying calm in stressful situations. I sat up and slid my legs out of the bed. "Arthur, I'm scared."

"Don't worry," I reached over and lifted the phone out of its charger and handed it to her. "Call the police. I'm going to see what's what."

"Arthur, no," she clasped my arm. "Don't go down there!" There was another thud from downstairs.

"You stay here," I freed myself from her. My blood rushed to my head as I stood up. I wobbled for a second before stepping forward. "Move the chair in front of the door after I've gone. Make sure you put it under the handle so it can't move." Dread washed over me, drowning out the fear. I had to make her stay here or something terrible would happen. "Promise me you'll call the police and stay here."

"Stay with me."

"Promise me!"

"I promise, Arthur," she dialled for the police. I opened the bedroom door and stepped into the hallway. The downstairs light was on. I could hear movement, someone walking through the house. I stopped at the top of the stairs. Molly had put an umbrella stand at the top of the stairs for my walking sticks. I kept leaving them downstairs and upstairs, so she had bought me several sticks and had them on both floors. I picked up a stick as quietly as I could, but it clanked against the china stand and the noise was loud in the otherwise quiet hallway.

I froze and waited, but the movement downstairs remained constant. I started down the stairs, ignoring the pain in my hip as I tried to go slowly and quietly.

At the bottom of the stairs, I blinked in the light and turned towards the kitchen where the noise was coming from. I headed closer and peered inside. There was a lone man, dressed in dark colours, a mask covering his entire face save for his eyes. He was searching through the drawers. Anger bubbled up inside, the dread and anger overwhelming my fear and making me bold. How dare he? How dare he come in here and try to steal from us? We, who'd worked hard for our entire lives. How dare he!

"You won't find nothing but cutlery in there, my lad." I lifted my stick. He leapt back away from me. I watched him for a moment as he took stock of me, his initial panic being replaced with confidence when he saw a small old man. I played up to his perception and leaned on the doorframe.

"Look, mister." He raised his hands. "I don't want to hurt you, but I need the money."

"I don't want to hurt you either. But I will, unless you leave right now."

"I can't leave," the man's voice sounded distant, like he was somewhere else, not present in the moment.

"Sure, you can. I won't press charges if you go now."

"Press charges?" His body language transformed when my words sunk in. He tensed, drawing himself up to his full height, and stepped forward, hands clenched into fists. "You think you'll press charges on me?"

"Calm down, lad." I held my ground but deliberately tried to look smaller, hunching my shoulders. I would have trembled if I could have done it convincingly. *Come on, you punk*, I thought, *I'm just a helpless old man with a bad hip and dodgy eyesight, come a little closer.* I gripped my stick, nice and firm.

"You're not going to do anything. Sit the fuck down, old man." He put his hand on the kitchen worktop and pushed the kettle, sugar pot, and tea bags onto the floor. The sound was loud, and I winced as the sugar pot shattered on the tile floor.

"That was my great aunt's." I raised my stick and swung down hard on his hand. The crack under my blow was satisfying, as was his scream, but I instantly regretted not aiming for something more vital than his hand. I should have known better. Broken fingers wouldn't stop him from attacking me, and as angry as I was, I could not overpower him.

I heard the bedroom door open and swore. Molly had promised me.

"Arthur?" she called. The man smiled through his pain at me.

"Your wife?" I lifted my stick again. He would not get past me.

"Who are you?" Molly's voice came from the upstairs landing. "What are you doing in my house?"

"Molly, go back to the bedroom!" I yelled.

"I'm the tooth fairy," a deep voice boomed from the upstairs hall. My arms turned to ice, numb and useless. There were two intruders.

"Get your hands off me!"

How dare they lay a hand on my wife! The flood of anger seemed to wash away my old age. I suddenly felt like I had in my twenties, strong, virile and, best of all, with military training. I moved smoother than I had in years and swung my stick with precision and strength. The boy in front of me crumpled, possibly dead. I didn't care. I turned and ran, something I'd not been able to do for years. While waiting for my new hip, I could barely walk. But now I was suddenly strong. I took the stairs two at a time. There was another man at the top of the stairs, pulling my Molly towards the top step, meaning to throw her down. Over my dead body, he would. I leapt over the last step and tackled him, wrapping my arms around his chest and hitting him with such a force that we both fell back away from the stairs, Molly fell with us. She cried out in fright and pain, but she was safe. She hadn't fallen down the stairs.

"You bastard." I raised my stick up. Somehow, I had kept hold of it. It was bloodied from my early altercation with the one downstairs. I brought it down hard and sharp and the body under me went limp.

I had done it. I had beaten them.

"Arthur?" Molly's hand touched my shoulder. "You did it, Art." I stood up and wrapped my arms around her tighter than I had in years. "You did it, Art. You saved me. I'm alive because of you. I'm always safe with you."

"Molly." My voice cracked. "I saved you. You're ok. I saved you."

I blinked as my vision faltered. I wasn't at home in the cottage; I was in the new bungalow. Molly wasn't safe. She was over a year dead. But in my hands, I clutched her pink dressing gown, bloodstained and smelling of her.

Chapter Two

I was sore when I woke up. It took several long minutes of gentle movement before I could convince my fingers to loosen up enough to let go of Molly's dressing gown and even longer for me to sit up.

The dressing gown was the one she had died in. My hands shook as I let go of it, and it fell to the floor. I thought they had destroyed it. Sophie had told me they had thrown it away. What was it doing here? Where had it come from?

My bones creaked as I rocked to my feet, and they were still creaking as I shuffled into the kitchen and switched the kettle on. I glanced at the sink and noticed there seemed to be more dishes than I remembered using waiting to be washed. I'd deal with them later.

The stiffness had eased a little by the time I reached the living room, tea in hand. I put the tea on the windowsill and picked up my grabber. Another gift from Sophie that had, much to my annoyance, turned out to be useful. A simple device, a stick with a claw on one end that I could operate from the other. I headed back to the bedroom where the dressing gown was on the floor. The grabber made picking up the gown easy. Lord knows, without it, I would have had to wait several hours for my back to ease up enough to bend down that far. Even then, there was never a guarantee I'd make it back to my feet by myself.

I had, until my diagnosis, thought the worst part of getting old was the fact I struggled to get up and down by myself. Suffice to say that the betrayal of my mind was much worse. The strong possibility that when I passed away, I wouldn't even know who the people at my bedside were was worse than a bad back.

I went back to the living room and stood by the window. Taking my tea in hand I looked out into the front garden and wondered again how Molly's dressing gown had turned up in my bedroom.

"You should plant hydrangeas, like we had at the cottage."

I almost dropped the dressing gown again as I turned behind me. Molly was sitting on the sofa, relaxed and smiling as if she'd spent the morning sitting there watching me faff about making tea. "I always loved the hydrangeas." She smiled at me. "You should get blue ones."

"Um… all right," I said, staring at her, my hands shaking. This was another hallucination. I'd had them all the time after Molly died. The medication stopped them. Had I forgotten to take my pills again? My heart stuttered when I realised that I couldn't remember the last time I had taken my pills.

"I bet if you ask Mike, he'll be happy to plant them in for you."

To suddenly see her again, so relaxed, not reliving that terrible night, it made my chest tight. She looked alive, alive and happy, chatting to me about flowers. I coughed, trying to shift the lump that had formed in my throat.

"Art?" she said.

I looked up, noting she was wearing her dressing gown. The same one I was holding. But now my hands were empty, and the blood was gone from the cloth.

"Are you all right?"

"Fine." I swallowed. "It's just… it's good to see you."

"I'm glad you think so." Molly laughed. "I haven't had time to tidy myself up yet today."

"You look beautiful," I said. My vision blurred, and I blinked away tears.

"Art, you're an old fool." She looked around at the living room. "I like the new home."

When I had had visions of Molly in the past, she had never really interacted with the surrounding world. It was something Dr. Wakefield had told me to pay attention to, to help convince me she wasn't real, that it was my broken mind trying to trick me. But here she was, commenting on my new bungalow. Her weight dented the couch cushions and her hair moved in the draft coming from the kitchen. I paused when I noticed that something was off. Molly's skin was grey. She was pale but not the pale of illness. She was actually grey. Molly noticed me staring and put her hand up to her face.

"You do?" I tried to distract her from my staring.

"Yes, it's small, but perfect. It has everything you could need. Sophie spent a lot of time trying to find you somewhere nice and close to her and Mike. I think she did marvellously." Molly beamed at me. How could this be happening? Molly couldn't really be here. It had to be the missed medication. The draft carried with it the smell of her perfume and I had to close my eyes. "Art did you hear me?"

"Yes, Sophie's a wonderful kid." I opened my eyes.

"She takes after her dad, taking care of everyone," Molly looked like she wanted to say more. But her smile faded and she looked away, as if she couldn't meet my gaze.

"What is it, sweetheart?" I leaned forward, all thoughts of Molly being real or not vanishing for a moment. I knew that look well. Something was upsetting her.

"Arthur." Something was wrong if she was calling me Arthur. "I hate this. I hate that I've tried so hard for so long to get you to see me. But now I'm here and rather than take a moment to talk, I need you to do something for me."

"What?"

"I need you to—"

"No, I mean what is happening? How are you here? Why now? How can I be sure this isn't just in my mind?"

"That's a lot of questions." Molly slumped a little, her shoulders dipping.

"You can't be surprised."

"No, I suppose not. I'll try and answer them." She took a deep breath. "I never left you, Art." My heart stuttered making my breath catch. "I've always been here, with you, you just couldn't see me until now."

"Why? Why now? Why not before?" I went to reach out but couldn't bring myself to completely close the distance.

"I don't know, I think it might have been the medication that doctor put you on, but I can't be sure. Just know that I would never leave you willingly, that's why I need you now. I wanted you to see me sooner, to have time to talk about how much I've missed you, but I can't. Time is running out for me. I need your help."

"How can I believe this?" I turned away. Concentrating I took several deep breaths and tried to focus on things I knew were real. The view out the window, the cup in my hand, it was smooth and warm. These things were real. I turned back to the sofa, half expecting Molly to be gone. She wasn't.

"I don't know what to say to you to make you believe me." She reached out, offering her hand to me. Putting the cup back on the window sill, I stepped forward and took her hand. She was cold, her skin was dry and fragile feeling, like it might come apart under a gentle pressure. I flinched back and let go.

"I need to take my medication." I turned and headed to the bathroom. My hands shook as I opened the medicine cupboard. The box of pills felt unreasonably heavy when I picked them up. How many had I missed? Did I mean to stop taking them? No of course not. I popped a capsule out of the foil.

"Arthur." Molly was behind me; I could see her reflected in the mirror. She looked so real. I had felt her skin under my hand. The same way I felt the cup I had been holding. "Arthur please don't. I don't have time for you to stop seeing me. I need you now." She was crying. Milky white tears fell down her face. I had made her cry. I was frightening her. Trying to abandon her again, just like I had on the night she died.

I put the pills back into the cupboard.

"You know I can never say no to you," I said.

"You're too good." Molly sniffed and wiped at her face. She took my hand again and led me back to the living room, sitting me down on the sofa she took her place beside me. "I'm sorry I haven't been here for you, that I haven't helped you with…" She struggled with her words before tapping the side of her head, referring to my illness. "You know I would have rather stayed with you. I would have helped you. We could have beaten it together."

"You don't beat dementia; you just fight as long as you can."

"You're still an old soldier," she leaned in and kissed my cheek. Her mouth was cold and there was a faint smell, like meat going bad. "But I mean it, I didn't want to go. I fought them with everything I had so I could stay with you. But it wasn't enough."

"Stop it. Don't apologise for dying, not for that."

"I just need you to understand that I didn't go easily."

"I know you didn't." There had been blood under Molly's nails, a sign she had fought her attacker tooth and nail. "But you did die. How can you be here now if you died then?"

"I told you I never left you, I was always there, just behind you." She took a deep breath. "I really didn't want to leave you. But now I need your help to leave."

"What?"

"I fought those men with everything I had and it wasn't enough I need you to fight them for me now." Her voice lost the trembling emotion and became harder. "I need you to fight them. I can't go where I'm supposed to go until they find justice."

"Molly, what?" I stuttered.

"The men who did this to me." I could hear the anger in her voice. "The ones who took me away from you."

"Molly, the police, they got him. He's in Blackwater, he'll be there for another thirty years," I said. "It's not right that he's alive when you're not, but we still got him."

"No Arthur, you only got one." I had a sudden memory of my dream, the feeling of panic when I realised that there were two men in the house.

"What?"

"The other one's still out, and everyone knows it," Molly said. "The police knew there was more than one man in the house that night, but they let him go."

"No, that can't be right."

"Arthur, I need you to do this for me," Molly came off the sofa and stood in front of me. I could smell her soap and the laundry detergent she had always favoured, but they didn't mask the undercurrent smell of marginally rotten meat. "I need you to find him. I can't rest until you do, and I'm running out of time."

"You're dead, girl. All you've got is time."

"No, I really don't." She held up greying hands. "If we don't do something soon, I won't look like myself. I'll start to look like my actual body, the one rotting in a grave. I've seen others who stayed and they, oh it's awful ..." She stopped, unable to go on.

"Something is wrong with you?" I set my hand on her knee. She was freezing cold. The foul smell was getting stronger.

"I don't want you to see me like that. What I'll look like in a few months, I won't look like me anymore. But it's more than that."

"What love?"

"If I'm stuck here then you'll leave me again."

"I would never!" The words choked out of me.

"You won't have a choice." Molly's voice was sharp, anger and grief warring in her tone. "Arthur, when you die, you'll move on, you'll go wherever the people who don't get stuck go. But I won't. I'm stuck. I can't move on until the people who killed me see justice."

"Molly, no." Bile rose in the back of my throat at the thought of losing her all over again, this time forever.

"Art, you're old, you're sick. As much as I hate to say it, you're going to die soon and when you do…" she trailed off before taking a deep breath. "You're getting sicker each day, every day things get a little bit harder, and soon you won't be well enough to help me. So no, I don't have all the time in the world. I have even less time than you do."

"What can I do?" my voice cracked as I spoke. I was an old man. I needed a stick just to walk. What could I possibly do?

"I don't expect you to go on a manhunt, Art." Molly laughed at me, her cool hand resting over mine on her knee.

"Then what do you want?" I said. "You know I'd do anything for you, but that won't bring you back."

"I know. I can't ever come back, but I can move on. But only if you help me. Please Art, I don't want to be trapped here, dead, forever."

"What can I do?"

"I need you to show people there were two men that night. He needs to be caught. But no one will believe you unless you can find proof." Her mouth pulled tight, her eyebrows drew down and her eyes were alight. It was a look I'd seen on her often, the expression she wore when she found a project and was ready to see it through.

"Proof?" I echoed.

"Yes," Molly said firmly. "I can help you with that."

"You can't help me if you're not real." Tears threatened again. How could this be real? She couldn't be real, she had to be a hallucination. I had been doing so well. Why couldn't I even manage a day without thinking about Molly and what had happened to her? Why couldn't I just remember the happy times? Why did I have to see her like this, lost, needing help and me unable to do anything because she was already dead? Why was I always so useless?

I turned away from her, intending to head back to the bathroom, back to the pills.

"Art," Molly snapped. I glanced at her. "I'm as real as I need to be, and you know it. Listen to your instinct, it's always led you right. It's telling you to listen to me." She reached out, wrapping fingers around my wrist. I felt her chill spread through me. Her grip was firm. How could she be a hallucination if I could feel her? I'd only ever seen and heard things before, I'd never been able to touch her. She was affecting the bungalow too the sofa dipped under her weight. If she wasn't real, would she be able to do that? No, she was real. She had to be.

My wife was here, and she needed my help.

"I'm listening." I sat next to her. Her hand went up to my shoulder before stroking round to the back of my head.

"The cottage was locked," she whispered. "No sign of forced entry."

"Then how?" I frowned.

"The key safe."

"The safe?"

My hip got really bad before the replacement, in the months before the operation I was effectively bed bound. Molly couldn't look after me by herself so the carers would come round twice a day to help with personal care and what not.

They put a key safe on the wall by the front door so the carers could get in without Molly or I having to let them in. That way Molly could come and go as she pleased and the carers could always get in. They kept the safe secure with a pass code that only the carers knew, and inside it was a key to our front door. They took the safe away after the operation, after Molly died, and I moved in with Sophie.

"Yes," Molly said.

"But no one ever said anything about damage to the safe."

"You're not thinking."

"I am," I insisted.

"No, you're not," Molly pulled me gently into a hug. I let her pull me forward and tried to not focus on the rotten smell under her soap. "The key was missing. The box wasn't damaged."

"You think they used the key to get in?" I pulled back from her.

"Yes."

"But…" I tried to think of an argument, but couldn't. It had been one of the chief points of contention, how the boy had gotten into the cottage. No one had figured it out. Molly had locked the windows and doors. There was no damage to any of them or the key safe. There were no footprints in the garden that weren't mine, and the boy who broke in hadn't said a word about how he'd managed it. It was like he had ghosted in and out.

"I locked the front door," Molly said. "I remember worrying about how the kids would get in if I overslept. They were going to pick me up in the morning to take me to see you." Molly let out a slow breath, her voice catching. "I was going to bring you the flapjacks you like, the small ones. I was going to give the grandkids some in the car."

"Shh." I tried not to think about how Sophie had been the one to find her mother, how Sophie had knocked and waited, then glimpsed her mother's body through the window at the foot of the stairs when Molly didn't answer. Molly should have gone quiet in her sleep. I should have been next to her in the bed, she shouldn't have been alone. Sophie shouldn't have had to find her mother like that. It was all so wrong.

"The key safe," I said again. "You think the carers had something to do with it?"

"Arthur?" I nearly fell out of my chair. Doris stood in the doorway, a covered plate in her hands. "Sorry, I didn't mean to make you jump. I did knock and the door was unlocked so..." Her expression was strained.

"Oh, um no bother, I was miles away, mustn't have heard you."

"Um," she shuffled in place. "Who were you talking to?" I glanced around the living room. Molly had disappeared.

"Oh, no one, just myself." I looked around again, Doris watched me intently. "It's a bad habit I picked up after Molly died." Doris smiled a little at my explanation.

"I know what you mean." She came into the living room properly. "I use Max as an excuse, I don't talk to myself you see, I talk to Max. Anyway, I brought you some breakfast. I thought after the move you might not have had a chance to go shopping beyond what your daughter did yesterday." She put the plate down and took off the cover. A good old English fry up was revealed and my stomach growled.

"You my dear are an angel." I smiled at Doris to show my appreciation and caught her blushing.

"Well, I never got out of the habit of cooking for two," she said as if making excuses.

"I never got into the habit of cooking full stop." I stood up and headed to the kitchen to get some cutlery. "Can I get you a tea?"

"No thank you," Doris called from the living room. "I can't stay, I've got some old girlfriends coming over. I just thought I'd drop this off for you."

"Very kind. Did you say the door was unlocked?" I came back into the living room and sat down.

"Yes," Doris was already heading out.

"Bugger, I thought I'd locked it. If I get broken into, it'll be my own fault."

"Oh, this neighbourhood is very safe. You shouldn't worry too much." She opened the front door. "Just pop the plate on my doorstep when you're done and I'll pick it up." With that she was gone.

The breakfast was delicious. Doris was a fantastic cook, not as good as Molly had been in my opinion but I'm biased. The bacon was crisp, the fried bread wasn't too greasy and the egg was runny. I finished the meal in moments, I hadn't realised how hungry I was until I started eating. I needed to get better at managing myself. When I put the cutlery down, I peered around the living room, looking for Molly.

"Molly?" I knew logically that she couldn't be real. I knew it. But God, I wanted so much for her to be here and the stab of grief I felt when she didn't answer me felt like she'd died all over again. I refused to let the grief overwhelm me. My wife had died over a year ago. I shouldn't be like this now. I hadn't been like this when my mother died when I was fifteen. I should get better at dealing with death, not worse.

"Dad?" Sophie's voice made me jump. I looked at the front door to find her standing there. "Are you alright? You look upset."

"No, I mean… um, I'm fine."

"Oh Dad, not another nightmare." Sophie came over to me. I couldn't look at her. I hated her seeing me like this. Her soft hand settled on my shoulder. "Maybe tell the psychiatrist, he might be able to prescribe something?"

"I'm already on enough drugs." Sophie opened her mouth as if to argue but stopped herself.

"Let's go. I've got the car outside." I looked at her and hated the expression I saw there. Pity, worry and exhaustion all mingled together on her face.

"Ok, just let me get dressed."

"I'm sorry, love," I said when we were in the car.

"Stop apologising. We're not even late."

"If I'd have been there that night…" I managed around the lump in my throat.

"Dad, stop," Sophie said. "If you'd have been there, then I'd have lost both of you. Losing Mum was the hardest thing that's ever happened to me. I don't think I could have handled it if I'd lost you too."

"There are days when I wish I had gone with her."

"Dad, please don't say that." Sophie's voice trembled. "Please don't."

"I'm sorry, love."

"Stop apologising," Sophie said. "None of this is your fault, not what happened to Mum, not the nightmares, your grief, the illness, none of it, so please stop apologising."

I said nothing. The car's engine rumbled louder as Sophie picked up speed only to brake as we approached a junction.

"What happened to Mum…" Sophie swallowed when we'd pulled out of the junction. "It was terrible, so terrible that sometimes I think it wasn't real. That kind of thing doesn't happen in our safe little town. No one is that terrible to do that to another person, let alone my mum, who was the kindest person. Hell, if the bastard had just knocked on the door, she probably would have had him in for tea and biscuits and given him the savings tin just to help him. You know, the police found out he was in trouble. He owed a lot of money to drug dealers and whatnot."

"Don't say that," I said. "Those bastards deserve nothing, not our pity or our understanding."

"Bastard, there was just one, Dad."

"No, there were two."

"In your nightmares, perhaps." Sophie didn't look at me. "Was it the same as before?"

"It was. There was one in the kitchen, a second one upstairs. Your mother, he pushed her down-"

"You know that's not what happened."

I nodded. The police report had said the boy had attacked Molly in the bedroom before running. She'd made it to the bottom of the stairs before collapsing. The boy they'd put away for it was barely twenty years old. A dumb kid, a stupid kid who'd made a mistake, they said. I knew better. He might have been young, but he wasn't stupid, and he wasn't alone. What they did had been deliberate. They'd planned it. Somehow they'd known she was old and alone and they'd gone in there to take what they could.

"Dad?"

"They wouldn't let me see her," I said as we pulled into the doctor's office.

"You know why." The men had hurt Molly badly. The doctors hadn't wanted me to see her, even the kids had made me stay away. Sophie had identified Molly for the police.

"I miss her," I said. Sophie sniffed and nodded, getting out of the car.

"I do too."

*****

"Molly woke me up again." I waited, expecting either a pitying sigh or irritation at my lack of progress. A hand settled on my shoulder, a brief pat before being withdrawn. Pity then.

"You're still dreaming about her?" the boyish doctor opposite me said. I rubbed my hand across my face to wipe away the sweat. Dr. Wakefield, waited quietly for me to answer. The words stuck in my throat, so I nodded instead.

"Still vivid?" he asked.

"I can smell her, hear her, and touch her. When I see her, it's like she never died." My voice cracked. I tried to cover it up with a cough.

"You're still taking the medication, aren't you?"

"Of course, I am." At least I was when I remembered to. Not having Sophie around to nag me meant I'd missed a couple of pills. Molly's claim that the pills stopped her from talking to me echoed in my memory for a moment.

"It's all right," he said. "Finding the right medication takes time. We can always try Rivastigmine."

"Already tried it, it gave me headaches and cramps in my legs." I leaned back a little in the chair. "I don't understand why all the different medications."

"We need to raise your brain's acetylcholine," my doctor looked at his computer screen.

"Fancy words, Doctor, I still don't understand you."

"I told you to call me Jim." Dr. Wakefield sighed. "Are you still seeing Molly when you're awake or only when you're dreaming?"

"It's only dreams now." I tried not to think about this morning. "But they are vivid. Vivid enough that sometimes when I wake up I don't realise I was dreaming until Sophie reminds me that Molly's gone. I hate it when they do that." Dr. Wakefield raised his eyebrows at me, and I hurried to explain. "Molly's gone and I don't get angry at my family for reminding me. It's the concern on their faces when they say it. Makes me feel like a foolish and cruel old man."

"What makes you say you're cruel."

"What makes you think I'm not?" I snapped.

"You miss your wife very much. Feeling embarrassed is normal; it's normal for someone who's suffered a loss like yours to struggle with it. Remind me, how long were you and Molly married?" He looked at me like he was testing me. He always got that expression when he asked me memory questions.

"Fifty-three years this October," I said promptly.

"That's a long time." The testing expression dropping, being replaced by an expression of professional empathy. "You must have been about sixteen when you got married?"

"Seventeen."

"And to lose her in such a violent way, it's hardly surprising it's caused an acceleration of..." Dr. Wakefield paused. "Sorry, I understand that you're not comfortable with the diagnosis yet."

"Nothing wrong with speaking the truth." I sniffed. "What happened to my Molly was violent and the only problem I have with my diagnosis is that you've told me I will end up dribbling in a corner, not knowing who I am anymore. No one would 'be comfortable' with that diagnosis."

"I don't think we put it quite like that. Plus, you've come so far in just a few months. The hallucinations have all but stopped; it's only dreaming now."

"Yes, but-" I managed before Dr. Wakefield interrupted.

"It's been barely a year. It isn't surprising that you're still dreaming about Molly or that we haven't quite got your medication spot on yet, but we will. You just have to give us time."

"Time is something I'm short of."

"Arthur-" Dr. Wakefield started.

"And it's not normal dreams," I said. "It's so real that I get up and go looking for her. I roll over in the bed expecting to hear her telling me she hears someone downstairs."

"Arthur." He gave me what I assume was supposed to be an understanding look, but it just appeared condescending. "It wasn't your fault what happened. I thought you had accepted that."

"I know it wasn't my fault." My fingers hurt when I gripped my stick hard. I might need a stick to walk, but my grip was still firm, my handshake stronger than the likes of Dr. "call me Jim" Wakefield.

"You're a poor liar. The reason you see Molly the way you do, it's partly because of your illness, but there's a large element of guilt involved."

"But I-"

"Every time you see her, you're reliving that night; you feel responsible for what happened. The dreams are your subconscious mind blaming yourself for what happened to her."

"She was my wife," I managed. "I was supposed to take care of her and I wasn't even in the house when she needed me." My hand was aching. I loosened my grip on the stick.

"You can't change the past." Dr. Wakefield leant forward.

"If I'd have been there, if I'd have put the operation off, or made Molly stay with Sophie while I was in the hospital..."

"Then things might be different," Dr. Wakefield said. "But you're only a man; you couldn't have known what would happen. It was not your fault."

I snorted, and Dr. Wakefield leant back in his chair with a sigh.

"I can only tell you the truth; it's up to you to be the one to accept it." He glanced at the clock before looking back at me.

"Looks like that's it for this week. But before you go, the move went well?"

I shrugged and stood up slowly, my joints complaining as I did so. Dr. Wakefield stood smoothly and held the door to the waiting room open for me as I walked out. "See you in a week, Arthur," he said as the door closed. I pulled a face.

"Dad!" Sophie snapped, standing up from her seat and setting the magazine she'd been reading aside. "Stop that."

"Hello, love." I smiled at her. "I thought you'd be in the car."

"Didn't think you'd get caught making faces at the doctor again, did you?" Sophie said. "This will only help if you take it seriously." She took my hand.

"That boy has some strange ideas."

"He's not a boy. He's in his thirties."

"He's got a little boy's handshake," I muttered as we walked out of the office to the car park.

Molly wasn't in the bungalow when Sophie dropped me off. Perhaps I had dreamed the whole thing? Molly was dead, she couldn't have been in the living room with me this morning. It was my foolish old mind breaking down. Tea, tea would help, I went to head into the kitchen. The knock at the door stopped me after a few paces. Frowning, I turned and went to answer it. When I opened it, I saw a warden, the warden who had stared at me the day before.

"Um, Mr. Webb." He couldn't hold my gaze for longer than a second or two at a time. "Is it all right if I come in? I wanted to talk to you."

"Sure," I said. "Can I get you something?"

"Oh, no, thank you." He sat on the sofa, I sat in my chair, and he fixed his eyes on the floor. "I wanted to come see you… I wanted to talk."

"About what?"

"Your wife," he said after swallowing loudly. My heart beat jack rabbit fast.

"What about my wife?"

"I knew her, my girlfriend. She was one of the carers who would come and help you guys. Her name was Donna."

"Donna," I said. "I think I remember a Donna,"

"She really liked Molly, I did too,"

"I thought I knew your face."

"Yeah, Donna got me in to help when your sink got blocked. My name's James."

"Yes, I remember." I could sort of recall his face. I remembered the sink being blocked and the carer, Donna, getting her boyfriend to help before we spent money on a plumber. Something in me, call it intuition, lit up at his words. I leaned forward, taking in his slight build and thin face.

"When I told you I could fix cars and needed work, you put me in touch with a friend of yours who owned the garage in town."

"Ahh yes." I nodded. "He never heard from you." The warden went red.

"Yeah." He rubbed the back of his neck. "Me and Donna, we broke up, and it hit me hard. I went off the rails, got into some old bad habits, then by the time I'd sorted myself out, I was too embarrassed to get in touch. My mum helped me get a job here. Mum lives next door to you as it happens."

"Doris?"

"That's her." James smiled. "Don't let her feed you any cakes, you'll be drunk after a single slice." He laughed but his humour faded quickly. "Um anyway, Donna and I are on good enough terms, which is nice. We've got a little boy. I see him every weekend." He pulled a photo out of his pocket and showed me a fat little baby, red faced and screaming. "He cries when you take his picture, every time."

"He's cu… angry." I was never good at lying.

"Yeah, got a lot of his dad in him." James continued to fidget. "But all that's behind me now and I got myself a room in a house share. Got the little man a cot to stay overnight. But Donna's not sure though. My housemates aren't her kind of people… they smoke a lot, not tobacco, and she's not into drugs."

"Good," I said. "No place for a baby around that sort of thing."

"I suppose."

"You're good to be out of it," I said. "Keep your nose clean and I'm sure you and Donna can find a way for you to spend more time with…"

"Harry."

"Harry, splendid name."

"Yeah, but these guys, the ones I live with, are my friends. They'd never hurt Harry. You stick by your mates, through thick and thin, right?"

"Friends are important." I said. "But family, especially your kids, they're more important."

"Good advice. I had a friend once. He was like a brother to me."

"Some friends can become family. Where's this brother now?"

"He's um, away." James shrugged. "He might get out soon, but not for a few years."

"I see."

"But I didn't come to talk about that. I came to talk about your wife."

"My Molly?"

"Yeah, she was a really nice lady and I'm really sorry for what happened to her."

"Yeah, she was."

"I uh…I was in Norfolk when it happened, I heard what… well, it was on the news. I'm really, really sorry. I mean, I can't imagine anyone wanting to hurt her on purpose, you know. At least they caught the guy who did it."

"Hm, I'm looking into that." I frowned at him. What an odd thing to say. Volunteering an alibi? Making assumptions about the motive? My heartrate picked up.

"What do you mean?"

"Just that I'm looking into it. That maybe there's more to what happened than the police know. I'm investigating myself."

"Have you found anything?" I didn't answer the question. The silence stretched for a long moment before James filled it. "News said it looked like an accident, burglary gone wrong. I bet the guy who broke in didn't mean to… well, it doesn't matter." What an odd thing to say.

"I guess not." The silence between us stretched long and felt heavy. Watching James fidget was irritating. I half wanted to yell at him to spit out whatever he wanted to say. Molly had always told me I had no patience with people. I bit my tongue and let the boy squirm. After a long few moments, his courage must have left him.

"Um." He stood up. "I'll come and see you tomorrow if you like, make sure you've got everything you need, that you're settling in."

"I'll be out all day tomorrow. I've got plans with my daughter, it's a family birthday."

"Oh." James' eyebrows rose and his expression softened, he looked oddly pleased at my comment. "Well, I'll make sure to come by soon. Goodbye, Mr. Webb."

"Goodnight." I watched him go before standing up and heading over to lock my front door this time.

Chapter Three

"Oh Dad, you look lovely." Sophie wrapped her arms around my shoulders. I jostled the bottle of wine I was carrying trying to prevent it from getting sandwiched between us. "Oh, what's that?"

"Just a bottle of red to go with lunch. The chap in the shop said it would go well with lamb." I handed Sophie the bottle and followed her inside. I toed off my shoes and sank my sock covered feet into the thick carpet. Sophie's home was bright and always smelled faintly of laundry soap. It was a beautiful home in its own way if a little bland, Sophie and Mike seemed to favour the colour cream. The walls were littered tastefully with pictures from holidays, just Sophie and Mike in the oldest ones then the newer ones with the addition of the grandkids. I walked past the living room door and spotted the two boys playing a racing game on the television. Sophie led me into the kitchen, a large, clean room of white and chrome.

"Hi, Art," Mike was putting sprigs of rosemary into a leg of lamb.

"Dad brought wine." Sophie opened the fridge.

"Nooooo!" Mike made a show of dramatically reaching for the bottle. "Never put red in the fridge."

"Oh… really?" Sophie said. "All wine goes in the fridge."

"Not red. We serve red at cellar temperature." Mike made a show of holding the bottle as if it were an infant. "Did that mean lady nearly put you in the fridge? Shhh, it's ok, I won't let her hurt you, don't worry." Sophie laughed and rolled her eyes as Mike took the bottle out to the utility room where it was cooler.

"Big kid," Sophie looked at me. "Are you sure you're up for visiting Mum?"

"Of course."

"Because you look exhausted." Sophie frowned. "We can always go in a couple of days."

"Granddad!" the shouts came from Simon and Oscar as they stampeded into the kitchen.

"Boys!" I narrowly avoided getting barrelled over. "You're getting far too big to be treating an old man this way. Six-year-olds should not behave this way." The boys both glared at me.

"I'm not six!" Simon, Sophie's eldest snapped. "I'm eight that's nearly as old as Daddy!"

"I'm seven!" Oscar yelled at the same time as his brother.

"Alright you two, calm down. Dad, I wish you wouldn't wind them up like that." Sophie reached out to pat Oscar's head. "Are you sure you're up for this today?"

"It's your mother's birthday, so we go today," I said firmly. "A little tiredness won't be the end of me. I'm made of much tougher stuff."

"I know you are."

"Can we come?" Simon asked. Mike smiled when I struggled to answer.

"Not today, I can take you to see your Gran tomorrow, like usual." Mike patted the boy's head.

"But why not today?" Oscar whined.

"Because today is just something for your mum and granddad." Mike stood up from the table. "Now you both help set the table and I might find it in my heart to let you back on the PlayStation this afternoon." The distraction technique worked like a charm. Both boys stood and started rapidly clearing the table.

"Well, I'm as ready as I'll ever be," I stood up. Sophie looked unsettled for a moment before her smile fell back into place.

"Great, let's go then." She headed out to the car. "You alright, Dad?" Sophie asked as I got into the car.

"Of course." We drove out of the cul-de-sac and into the town. I stared listlessly out of the window, watching the town crawl past.

"We should stop for coffee first," Sophie said. "I missed mine today."

"Alright, I didn't make tea this morning either." I let Sophie assume it was because of the day, rather than the fact I hadn't been able to find the tea bags that morning. No matter how much I tried, I couldn't remember where I put them, and they weren't in the places you'd expect. I must have put them somewhere, but damned if I knew where.

We pulled up to a coffee shop, and I frowned.

"We don't normally——" I started.

"I know, but I thought it would be appropriate," Sophie interrupted. "But first." Sophie pulled me with her as she walked down the high street, muttering about getting flowers first. I swallowed the lump in my throat—I had almost forgotten the flowers. I picked tulips. Molly had always liked tulips. Sophie followed suit, getting a different coloured bunch.

We went back to the coffee shop, and I hesitated before going inside.

"You know we don't have to go in here," Sophie said. "It was a bad idea."

"No, it wasn't." I stepped forward and held the door open. "It's right to be here on this day."

I watched as Sophie went to the counter, trusting her to get the drinks and possibly a cake. I found a small table by the window.

"It's changed a bit," Sophie came over from the counter. "They've redecorated."

"I hadn't noticed. The chairs have been redone, though."

"Mum would have liked the new colours."

"I never understood why she favoured this place over the one further down," I admitted. "But she always did. She loved this place."

"Yeah." Sophie looked out of the window. "Do you think we should have done another trip this year?" she asked suddenly.

"What?"

"Last year, for Mum's birthday. Going away felt weird, but now I'm thinking we should have done it again."

"The Isle of Man, again?"

"It was nice to celebrate her birthday by visiting there. Even if part of me felt like we were leaving her here while we all buggered off on a trip."

I shrugged and took a sip of my tea. "It was a pleasant trip. I kept telling her we should go somewhere else. There was an enormous world to see, but she always wanted to keep going back there."

"Visiting the grave today feels poor in comparison," Sophie said.

"I don't like graveyards. Pointless places."

"They are places to remember."

"I don't need to go to a grave to remember your mother."

Sophie nodded. "I know. But we'll do it, anyway. Either Mike or I bring the boys up there every couple of weeks. We keep it nice."

"That's good," I said, not sure what else to say. Molly's body might be under the earth in the cemetery, but she wasn't. I tensed when I looked over at a table closer to the door. Molly was sitting, watching us. She had a stiff smile fixed in place. "We should go." I finished my tea.

"Ok." Sophie picked up the cups and took them to the counter before we headed out.

The graveyard was a chilly place. Even in the summer, it always felt chilly here. For the first time today, I was glad of my suit. The damn thing was too tight and scratchy as all hell, but it kept me warm. We walked silently through the raised stones until we reached a pure white one. It was a little smaller than the others. Molly had never been one for flashy, attention-grabbing things. The small stone suited her.

"Hi Mum, happy birthday." Sophie leaned down and put the flowers into the small metal vase built into the stone. Taking mine from me, she did the same. Molly stood several yards behind us and watched.

"Happy birthday, love," I looked at Molly, not the stone. She nodded once at me.

"Dad," Sophie said, still kneeling by the stone. "Is something going on?"

"What?"

"You've been strange for a while now. I know you've been trying to cover it up but you're a terrible liar."

"Nothing's going on." I flinched when Sophie looked up at me, crying.

"You're lying again. Even here, I thought you might be honest if I asked you here."

"There's nothing going on." Sophie glared at me and stood up. "I don't want to fight. Not here, not today."

"I don't want to fight either." I reached up and brushed a tear away with my thumb. "Please don't worry about me, pet."

"I can't not worry. You're my dad."

"Exactly. I'm the one who worries about you."

"Yes, but I'm not the one who's lying." Sophie pushed my hand away gently. I took a deep breath; she was right, I shouldn't lie."

"I hate these places," I looked out over the graveyard. "Pointless, spooky places."

"I know. You always say Mum isn't here, just the body she left behind when she was done with it."

"She wasn't finished with it. They forced her out of it." I took a deep breath. I didn't want to be angry today. "But I meant what I said. That's not your mum under the ground."

"I know."

"Because she's over there." I gestured to Molly, still several yards behind us.

"Dad?" Sophie went a shade paler. I looked away while she figured out what I meant. She took my hand and squeezed hard. "Not again. Since when?"

"Couple days now. She's different this time."

"Different?"

"Before she was always…" I stopped. I had never told the family what I saw exactly, only that I could see Molly. That's when they'd made me go to a doctor and I'd been diagnosed with dementia.

"Dad?"

"Before she was always stuck in a loop, never reacting to what was really happening, just doing the same thing repeatedly, it was easier to say she wasn't real. But this time, she's different."

"I don't understand." Sophie's voice was shaking.

"She's real, Sophie. She talks to me. She moves things in the bungalow, keeps putting things away where I can't find them. I say things and she reacts. She asks me to do things for her. She's… real, I'm sure of it."

"Dad." Sophie was crying harder this time. "Dad, she's not real. Mum died over a year ago."

"I know. I know that and so does she." Sophie took my hand, and we started back towards the car.

"You need to speak to the psychiatrist again, we need to get him to look at your medication."

"I…" I stopped. Sophie wasn't going to believe me and I couldn't blame her. It was foolish of me to say anything to her. She was only going to worry.

"Dad." I looked at her. "Promise me you'll talk to him." I swallowed and nodded.

"Do you want tea?" Sophie asked when we arrived back at her house. I shook my head. "Dinner shouldn't be too long, maybe half an hour."

"In that case, do you mind if I lie down for a moment? I've been getting woozy lately."

"Of course, are you alright?" Sophie looked immediately concerned, and I felt a pang of guilt.

"I'm fine, sweetheart." I forced a smile. "Just all the excitement with the move and whatnot I think. It's tired me out."

"The guest bedroom has clean sheets. I'll call you five minutes before we eat." I headed out and upstairs.

I walked past the guest room into Sophie's office. I could taste the bile at the back of my throat, it rose every time I lied to someone I loved. But Molly's words rang in my mind; I had to find out if what she had said was true, if there was evidence in the police file that the intruders had been nursing staff.

Sophie's office was small but well organised. She had her mother's tendency for organisation. It was the reason we'd got a copy of the police file. Sophie, in her endless proficiency, had requested it when the case had been concluded. It wasn't the complete file, sensitive information and whatnot was blacked out, but it was everything they could legally give us.

I opened the small filing cabinet and peered inside. Nothing was labelled, which surprised me. But then, why would it be? This was Sophie's cabinet. Why would she label it for other people? The taste of bile rose again as I reminded myself I was snooping through my daughter's files to see if she had concealed the truth from me.

I started thumbing through the neatly divided rows of papers, bills, the car agreement, the mortgage and extension paperwork, all private documents that had nothing to do with me. I tried not to notice them and concentrated on locating the police documents.

I found it after a few moments, neatly filed at the back of the second drawer. Pulling it out, I flicked through it quickly. I considered taking it with me. I could read it more carefully at home, but if Sophie noticed it was gone, how would I explain me having it? It was bad enough my snooping without Sophie knowing I was snooping.

The file was big. Most of the information I skipped, including the autopsy report. I wanted nothing to do with that. Instead, I focused on statements. There were several statements from the officers that had been called to the cottage. I had to stop halfway through the first one and take several deep breaths. If I went downstairs looking upset, then it would be immediately obvious I had been doing something other than resting. I waited for a moment to calm down before continuing. Reading the story of how the officers had arrived at the bungalow, had noted Molly prone on the floor by looking through the window and breaking down the front door. Noting the extent of her injuries. It wasn't easy reading.

I turned to a second statement, this one from the officer who had searched the property. Nothing much of note there save for the level of damage, though there was a note of no sign of forced entry and the front door was locked when the police arrived.

The forensic documents were more fruitful. I nearly dropped the file when I read, "Two sets of unidentified fingerprints," and again when I saw, "Two footprints in the garden, size 9 male and size 11 male." Neither of those were mine. I was a size 8. I kept looking, scanning witness statements, noting one from the carer who had come in the day before. They mentioned they hadn't realised I'd gone into the hospital, hence them attending when I wasn't there. I nodded to myself. It had to have been the carers, they knew Molly was alone, they had access to the property, there was evidence of multiple people in the cottage that night.

Molly was right.

"Dad, are you awake?" Sophie called up from downstairs.

I flinched with surprise. Had it been that long already? "I'll be right down."

"Hurry," Mike shouted. "I want to open this bottle of red!"

I folded the forensic documents and put them in my pocket, replacing the rest of the file back into the cabinet. Sophie would notice the entire file going missing, but a few pages was unlikely.

Downstairs, the table had been set as if it was Christmas. The fancy tablecloth saved for best occasions was out and the expensive crockery laid for six. The extra place setting was deliberate. At the head of the table, they had set a place for Molly, with a framed photograph of her in place of a plate. Apparently, this was a family tradition in Mike's family; on birthdays for those we had lost, a place would be set for them. His grandmother had started the tradition years ago, and they still did it to this day. Sophie had liked it and insisted we do it as well.

"Dad." Sophie handed me a plate and gestured for me to help myself to the array of dishes laid down at the centre of the table, while Mike cut the meat.

"This looks fantastic, Mike," I said around the lump in my throat, my mind still on the document resting uncomfortably in my pocket.

Mike grinned. "You think buttering me up will get you extra portions?"

"Worth a shot."

"It was successful." He put two slices of meat on my plate.

We ate the meal together, making small talk, mostly about Simon's and Oscar's school and friendships. I smiled as the boys talked animatedly about who was best friends with whom and who was better at this sport or that. It was a lively meal; Molly would have enjoyed it. I tried to ignore the forensic papers weighing heavily in my pocket.

I didn't stay long after dinner was done, long enough to be polite, but one benefit of being old is that no one bats an eyelid when you want to go to bed early. Sophie drove me home in silence. I kept glancing at her as she drove. Her hands gripped the wheel too hard, her face was tight with tension.

"Can you drop me at the gate? I could use the short walk." I patted my stomach.

"Mike always makes too much food." Sophie pulled up at the 'village' entrance and stopped the car. "Dad, I want you to tell Dr. Wakefield."

"I already have."

"Exactly what you told me today?"

"Maybe not exactly."

"Well, I want you to do it, or I will." She took my hand. I met her eyes. "I love you. I don't want to lose you."

I wanted to promise her she wouldn't lose me, but I couldn't because it was inevitable. I was going to die one day, long before her. But the thought that she might lose me before I died turned my stomach.

"I don't want you to lose me either, I'll talk to the doctor." I got out of the car. I watched her drive away before turning and heading up the hill to my bungalow.

"Why do they always build these villages on bloody hills?" I grumbled to myself. "Five different places and every single one was built on a hill or up a hill." I continued to grumble to myself all the way back to the bungalow.

The darkness changed the look of the place. What in daylight seemed to be cutesy non-descript bungalows warped in the darkness into indifferent squat hollows. Shadows loomed, broken only by puddles of bright orange light.

A spike of panic made me stop. With everything so dark, I did not know which bungalow was mine. My heart rate picked up as I tried desperately to recall what my front garden looked like.

"Art, is that you?" Doris' voice called out of the gloom. I turned to see her several houses back. I'd walked right past the bungalow.

"Oh, um yes." I turned and headed back.

"You're out late," Doris smiled. "It's too cold to be out this late."

"My daughter dropped me off. I was at hers for dinner."

"Oh, that's nice." Doris' smile faded and her brow creased. "I saw you walk right past the window when I was in the kitchen. I was worried you'd gotten lost." My face felt hot from embarrassment.

"Oh well, you know how it is. All these damn places look the same in the dark." Doris looked around, her expression a mixture of unconvinced and concern.

"Well," she said after a long moment. "You're home now. Oh, before I forget I think my boy was looking for you earlier today, he's one of the warden's here. I saw him in your garden, if you've been out all day you might want to give him a call tomorrow, see what he wanted." I glanced at my bungalow. In the window stood Molly, her face twisted in terror. Her hands pounded on the window as she mouthed my name.

"Molly," I stepped forward, nearly pushing Doris aside as I did so.

"Oh um, well, goodnight," I heard Doris say as I charged up the path as fast as my frustratingly frail body would allow.

I opened my front door and froze.

The living room was a disaster, ornaments and trinkets knocked off shelves, furniture tipped over, even the sofa had been upturned, the cushions torn. But the biggest upset was the wall unit; it had fallen forwards. The books it held were littered across the floor. Broken ornaments lay spread around it. They had pulled one drawer out, the papers it had contained were scattered.

"Someone's broke in. Molly!" I raced through the bungalow as fast as I could manage. "Molly!" I called out. "Molly, where are you?"

"Art!" The relief in Molly's voice made my stomach roll. She crept out of the bathroom and started crying the moment she saw me. "Oh, Art, thank God." She stumbled towards me, visibly trembling. I went to her, wrapping my arms around her. She was ice cold to the touch and where her cheek touched mine was clammy. The smell was worse. My grip on her wavered. I almost pushed her away with revulsion as that smell rose. Molly clung tighter to me and guilt rose, beating the revulsion down. How could I push her away? Even if it was a gut reaction? How could I let this happen to her? It was getting worse because I wasn't acting fast enough. I was failing her again.

"What happened?" I said after a moment.

"He knows." Molly was weeping. "He must be watching you. He knows you're looking for him."

"Who?"

"Art, it was him," she insisted. "He was looking for the papers."

"The file is at Sophie's house. All I have are these." I fumbled in my pocket for the forensic report I had stolen. A stab of cold knifed through me. "What if he goes to Sophie's?" I let go of Molly and turned to go to the phone. Sophie picked up on the second ring.

"Sophie." I said, my voice high pitched and obviously panicked. "Is your door locked?"

"Dad, what?"

"Is your door locked?" I snapped.

"Yes, it always is. What's wrong?"

"You need to call the police, right now. Someone is coming, someone dangerous."

"Dad what are you talking about?" Sophie spoke quickly. "Dad are you alright?"

"I'm fine, you need to call the police, he's already on his way!"

"Dad you're not making sense. What's wrong? Who's on his way?"

"The person who killed your mother, he's been here and now he's coming to yours, I need you to call the police."

"What do you mean he's already been there? Dad is someone with you?" I looked at Molly who shook her head slowly.

"She's not going to listen." Molly put her hand on my shoulder and squeezed gently.

"Oh." My mouth was suddenly dry. Molly was right. "Um, sorry dear." I tried to slow my words, to make myself sound calm. "I'm sorry, I just had another nightmare. It was very realistic. I'm sorry."

"Oh Dad, thank god." Sophie let out a long breath. "You scared me."

"I'm sorry." I didn't know what else to say. My chest felt tight. The thought of him coming to Sophie's house, breaking in with her and the boys there. It made me sick to my stomach. "I didn't mean to frighten you."

"Don't worry." Sophie said, the relief fading from her voice. "Maybe have something to drink and try and go back to sleep. If you have a nightmare again though I'm only on the end of a phone." Her voice was getting tight, as if she was getting upset.

"I know, thanks love." I hung up.

"They'll never believe you. You can protect them by finding him. He won't go after them until he's got you. They need you to catch him."

"But I'm a foolish old man. No one's going to listen to me."

"They will if you get proof." She was suddenly calm. "You underestimate yourself, Arthur, you're the smartest of us all, the bravest too. I know you'll know what to do." I took a deep breath.

It was time to stop messing around. Time to take this seriously. Molly needed me; Sophie needed me. I would keep them all safe this time.

Swallowing the panic building in my stomach, I turned and headed to the bedroom to pull the cord that would summon the wardens.

*****

"Sophie, calm down," I said.

"But Dad, you've only been there a few days, and someone has broken in." Sophie's voice was shaking. "And only a few hours ago you told me you'd had a nightmare, not that someone had broken in!"

"Calm down, love." I moved out of the way of a warden.

"Mr. Webb." James tapped my shoulder. I put my hand over the receiver. "The police are all done, so we're going to get on with the tidy up."

"Thank you." I turned back to the phone. "The police are done, love. If there's anything to find, they will have found it."

"That's not the point. Someone broke in."

"The wardens said the house has been empty for a couple of weeks." I kept an eye on the wardens fixing up the bungalow.

"And?"

"And apparently, that means it's vulnerable. God knows why, though, what's to steal from an empty house? Either way, it hardly matters - I'm fine."

"But Dad!"

"This was just terrible luck."

"Terrible luck." Sophie sighed. "That's one way to put it. But I'd feel better if you stayed with us tonight."

"It's very late. The kids are in bed, and I'm not comfortable with you driving so late. Besides, I'm fine. The wardens are getting a locksmith over in the morning."

"But you know stress can make your illness worse; it's why we were hesitant to move you in the first place and after what you told me earlier-"

"I'm fine, Sophie," I said, as firmly as I could manage.

"But-"

"No, no buts. Stop worrying." I heard her sniff. "I'm sorry Sophie; I'll call you first thing in the morning, ok?"

"Ok, Dad," she sniffed again. "I don't mean to nag, I just worry."

"I know you do." I sighed. "I wish you wouldn't; I'm your dad. I'm the one who's meant to worry."

"Yeah, ok. I'll speak to you in the morning. First thing, though."

"Ok, first thing." I put the phone down.

"You boys ok?" I called into the living room.

"Yes. Mr. Webb, we're almost done."

"You want a drink?"

"No thank you," the call came back.

"Well, I bloody well do," I muttered and reached up to the cupboard. I pulled a glass down and tried to ignore my shaking fingers. Another break-in, another one. Despite what I had said to Sophie, the idea that my home had been invaded again made my stomach turn. I walked out to the living room and lifted a bottle out of the globe, the only thing untouched in the living room, and poured a glass.

"You boys sure?" I asked, watching as the two wardens picked up what was left of the mess. Amazingly, only a few ornaments had been broken in the invasion. The wall unit had a few new scratches, but the damage was slight. Even the TV had survived, with only a few scratches to show for its ordeal.

"See anything missing, Mr. Webb?" the warden I hadn't met before asked. He was a tall fellow and towered over James. I shook my head.

"Nothing that I've noticed."

"You alright there? You're very pale. Want me to call the doctor?" James asked.

"No, lad." I sat in the armchair, my legs feeling weak. "I'm ok, just old memories."

"I bet you've seen some things?" the other warden said, his voice strained, but he was obviously attempting to sound as light-hearted as possible.

"Shut the fuck up," James snapped. I held up my hand. "Sorry, Mr. Webb."

"What'd I do?" the tall warden asked.

"Nothing lad," I said. "You're right though, I have seen worse, a lot worse than some busted ornaments and some upside-down furniture."

"But why break in and not take anything?" James said.

Again, I saw the old cottage, the furniture knocked over, the TV missing and the blood on the bedroom carpet. Molly's words echoed; he was looking for something. My earlier feeling of suspicion at James was fading. The man looked as confused as I felt and he seemed so genuine, like his concern and confusion were heartfelt. I didn't know what to think. I knocked the whisky back and grimaced.

"I don't know." I stood up. "This needs ice." I walked into the kitchen.

Opening the freezer, I could hear James and his co-worker talking.

"Have you looked at him? A strong wind would knock him over; there's no way he could have pulled that great big unit down."

"But the police said there was no damage to the door or any of the windows; you saw the alarm hadn't gone off either; no one broke in here."

"These old guys forget to lock their doors all the damn time. Half the time when I'm called out, I don't even have to use our key."

"But why not take anything? Why just make a mess? I'm telling you this was not a break-in." There was a moment of quiet. "You know how the sick ones get. Last year we had the old boy who caved his missus' head in, some of them get violent."

"Did you look at him? He's shaking just from the effort of standing up."

I filled the glass with ice and, making a deliberate noise so they would know I was coming back, walked back out to the living room.

"You boys have done plenty." I sat down again. "Don't worry about the rest; I'll run the Hoover round in the morning."

"You sure, Mr. Webb? I don't mind, it won't take me a moment," James said.

"I'm sure, lad." I kept my gaze on my glass. These boys thought I had done this myself? Illness or no, why the hell would I do that? Wasn't it obvious? Someone was looking for something, looking for evidence against themselves.

"Alright then, but don't forget we're just a call away, or just pull the red cord and we'll be back in a moment," James said, heading towards the front door.

"I'll do that. Don't forget the lock, please." The satisfying click of the lock falling into place let me relax a little.

They had put the remote control on the coffee table. Reaching forward, I grabbed it and flicked on the news to drown out the silence. I watched one of the familiar faces of the local news team as they talked enthusiastically about a new exhibit at the museum. I drifted off to the museum curator, explaining about Mayan culture.

I woke up abruptly. A frigid hand rested atop my own. I looked down and swallowed the lump in my throat.

"Molly," I looked up. She was sitting on the sofa wearing her pink nightgown, free of bloodstains. It reminded me of when the grandkids had picked it, it looked like something you'd expect the grandma in Little Red Riding Hood to have worn. I used to tease her, threaten to buy her a bonnet.

"Arthur." She snivelled. "Oh God, what do I do if something happens to you?"

"It's alright Molly," I reached out to her and pulled her to me. "It's alright. You're safe with me."

"I'm going to end up stuck here forever, Art," she gripped me tightly.

"No pet, I'm here, it will be ok."

Chapter Four

I sat in front of Dr. Wakefield, not making eye contact and trying to will myself to stop the nervous sweating.

"It's alright, Arthur, there is no need to apologise," Dr. Wakefield said.

"I was late. At the very least, you deserve an apology." I almost hadn't come to the appointment at all but decided not attending would raise more suspicion. But I couldn't stop the nerves if Dr. Wakefield cottoned on to what was happening, or if I let something slip, he'd think my disease was getting worse, he'd put a stop to what I was trying to do. He'd stop me from helping Molly.

"Which you have given twice now, and I have accepted." Dr. Wakefield sighed. "Can you tell me why you're late?"

"I've...It's nothing." Dr. Wakefield stared at me in silence. I tried to stare him out, but felt my resolve crumble quickly. "I've been having trouble lately."

"It's not because you don't want to attend our appointments anymore?"

I shook my head. "I won't lie to you, Dr. Wakefield. I did not start attending these appointments of my choice."

"I know it was your daughter who encouraged you."

"Even now, after so long, our appointments are not my favourite thing, but I can see the benefit. I am making some improvement, I suppose."

"That is good to hear," Dr. Wakefield said. "It has been apparent to me you've been making progress for a while now and it is good that you have realised this."

"I know that these appointments have helped me. I want to continue with them. I've just not been as well organised as I used to be."

"Any trouble with the clocks?" Dr. Wakefield asked. My eyebrows rose before I could stop myself. "Ah."

"Molly was always the one who remembered the birthdays, the dentist appointments." I shrugged. "I just woke up each day and did as she told me."

"Much like when you were in the Air Force?" I think he was trying to be funny, but it was accurate.

"A bit more peaceful than RAF. Molly had a much softer way of telling me where I needed to be." I chuckled. "But she was a firm soft. She could have led entire divisions into war and kept them all fed and watered without so much as breaking a sweat."

"I've said it before, Arthur; sounds like your Molly was a wonderful woman."

"She was. You wouldn't want to cross her, though. She'd have your lungs for earrings if you crossed her." I sighed. "She certainly kept me in line."

"It is not surprising that you miss her."

"Yes, well, not as much as I used to." My heart stuttered when I realised what I had said. Dr. Wakefield watched me.

"It's alright, Arthur," he said after a few moments. "You can speak freely here; everything is completely confidential."

"I had another break-in." I changed the subject. "The living room got ransacked."

"What?" Dr. Wakefield's eyebrows shot up. "Another break-in? Arthur, are you alright?"

"Yes, I was out. Again."

"Good, well not good, but it is good you were not there."

"The wardens don't think anyone broke in," I said. "I'm not sure what they think happened, but I heard them talking."

"Were the police called?"

"Of course, but they couldn't find anything missing and no evidence that anyone entered through force. They just gave me a crime number and told me to change the locks." We were quiet for a long moment.

"You've been managing well until..." Dr. Wakefield paused and glanced at his oversized diary. "The last few months; you've been late several times over the last six months, even when you were making progress during the appointments."

"I have apologised."

"You misunderstand. I don't mean to criticise; I am merely concerned, especially considering what you just told me."

"Concerned?" I snorted. "I'm hardly the first old man whose wife kept him in line. Molly did everything. I could barely make a cup of tea when I moved in with Sophie. Can you imagine having to get your own daughter to teach you how to use a washing machine?"

"You're not the first to struggle after such a loss, not the first to struggle at all." Dr. Wakefield closed his diary and put his papers to the side.

"I sense a but coming."

"Yes, well." He took a deep breath. "I am pleased with your progress, but I am concerned about your deterioration."

"Deterioration? I thought I was progressing!" Dr. Wakefield nodded and watched me carefully; I had the sudden impression he expected me to bolt, as if I could.

"You are overall, but I want to suggest something," he said. I shuffled in my seat under his intensive scrutiny.

"Oh, yes?" I waited for the suggestion of an in-home carer or a full-time nurse.

"I want you to go for some tests," he said.

"What tests?" I was fed up with tests, blood tests, liver function tests, and lung function tests. It felt like the minute you turned sixty, they started waiting for you to fall apart and started draining all your blood to monitor it.

"I would like to send you for a couple of blood tests, and if the results are what I expect, then I would like to send you back to the neurologist."

"Neurologist? Why would you send me to a neurologist? Speak plainly, doctor."

"We could always do another MMSE test here." I frowned at him and stood up. If he would not be clear, then I saw no point in remaining. "Please Arthur, sit down. I want to see if the dementia is advancing."

"Advancing." My legs shook and I all but collapsed back into the chair. I had a vision of being surrounded by Sophie, Mike, and the grandkids. Me lying there, being afraid, not knowing who they were. "But, I'm fine. It's just the stress of the move and another break-in."

"I know. I think you could be right. That's why I want blood tests first. I want to get your GP to check your thyroid hormones and your B12 levels. I'll ask him to do some checks."

"I don't understand." I swallowed. "Forgetting a few appointments doesn't mean I'm getting worse already."

"Of course it doesn't, but if your disease is advancing or something else is going on and we find it early, then we've got a better chance of slowing the progression or dealing with the issue."

"I'm not getting worse."

"If it's something simple like your vitamin B12 levels, then it could be a matter of introducing a supplement or perhaps a short course of injections," Dr. Wakefield said softly. "But I wouldn't be doing my job properly if I didn't request tests."

"Ok. Do your tests."

*****

I shambled through town after my appointment, heading towards the bus stop. The streets were quieter than when I had been a boy, but that's not to say they were quiet. I tried not to let the crowd hurry me along. The hustle and bustle of town life had changed over the years. People still walked the streets, but they did so with a frantic purpose these days. I shuffled along lost in my memories of when I would walk down this street with Molly and Sophie, one of the charity shops on the high street used to be a newsagent, Sophie would always insist on going in for sweets in the winter and 20 pence ice creams in the summer.

I was so lost in thought that I didn't realise until I looked up that I had walked right past the bus stop. I was nearly at Molly's favourite coffee shop. I stopped walking and heard a person behind curse and skirt around me. I considered turning around and heading to the bus stop, properly this time. But tea and a slice of cake sounded nice. I'd skipped breakfast this morning after not being able to find bread for the toaster and losing patience with myself. So why not get some cake?

Molly was waiting for me at the table by the window when I arrived. I bought tea and a small cake and headed over to her. Molly was worse than before; her skin was grey and hanging on her cheekbones like old leather, thin and fragile. Her eyes were milky and surrounded by dark circles. Her hair was thinning and falling out. I could see her scalp. My stomach rolled, and I wished I hadn't bought the cake.

"Art." She smiled at me. "I'm glad you started coming here again. I love it here."

"Why?" It was hard to look at her. This was my fault. Here I was having tea and cake and she was getting worse.

"The cakes were always perfect," she said. Then frowned. "You look troubled."

"Of course, I'm troubled," I kept my voice down. "Look at you." Molly fussed with her hair for a moment and another clump fell free. My throat felt suddenly dry. Now, as if things weren't bad enough, I'd made her feel self-conscious. I reached out and took her hand. "You're beautiful."

"Don't lie Art. I know what I look like."

"I don't care, you're still my girl and to me, you're always beautiful. I just… I can't bear to see you suffer because I'm not good enough."

"I'm sorry to have put more on you," she pulled her hand free. Her dry skin flaked as she did so.

"Dr. Wakefield thinks the disease is getting worse and is sending me for tests. I'm running out of time to help you." I tried to refocus the conversation.

"You can do it. But you were right about time. I am running out of time. Soon I'll be stuck and this." She gestured at herself. "It will keep getting worse. I can't bear that thought."

"I can't either. I'll fix this, Molly, don't you worry, I'll sort it all out."

"You need to hurry." Molly reached up to cup my face. "You're close to the end now."

"Don't say that."

"You know I'm right," she said. "You can feel it. Every day the real world gets further away from you. If only you'd gone to the doctors sooner."

"Hah."

"They can slow it down. Art, many people live well with sickness, but you waited too long,"

"Wakefield says it slowed down."

"And it has, but it's still marching forwards. Every day it gets closer and everything else gets further away. That's why Sophie cries when she sees you now."

"I won't let her see me fade." I angrily stabbed into the cake with my fork, swallowing it down with force. "Once you're taken care of, I'll set myself up somewhere safe before it's too late. She won't know where it is. She won't have to see me that way."

"There's my brave solider. It's the right thing to do. Keep away from them. Don't let them see you like this."

"I'll be alright if I know you're safe."

"Thank you. But what do you plan on doing next?"

"I'll go talk to the police; they won't do any bloody good, but it's the only thing I can think of now."

"Finish your tea first," Molly coaxed. She watched patiently while I finished the cake and downed the tea. I waved to the waitress as I stood up and nodded my thanks as she headed over to clear my table.

The streets still felt frantic when I stepped outside, but the hustle and bustle eased when I got off the high street and headed down to the police station. The station was in a big old building near to the library, thankfully it wasn't far. The day was bright and sunny but the wind felt cold and after only a few minutes I was wishing I'd brought my hat. Molly followed behind me, a silent presence seen by none but me.

When I reached the station, I took a moment to run the chill from my hands before heading to the reception.

"How can I help?" the junior clerk behind the reception asked.

"I'd like to see Inspector Hoffman if he's got a moment? My name is Arthur Webb."

I watched as the clerk called through to the inspector and was surprised when he hung up and told me to take a seat. I was expecting to be sent away with an appointment if I was lucky. I waited. Forty-five minutes later, the inspector came into reception and called me through.

"I understand it was Molly's birthday recently," he said when we sat down in the small interview room.

"I'm surprised you remember."

"I can't help but remember certain files, certain people, and Molly sticks in my mind."

"As she should," I firmed up my voice. I had to make him listen. He had to see that I was right.

"Well, what can I do for you, Mr. Webb?"

"Thank you for seeing me without an appointment," I started. "I wanted to talk to you today about Molly, in particular, what you're going to do to find the second man."

"Second man?"

"Yes, I've seen the file. There is evidence of two people that night and only one is in jail. I want to know when you think you'll find the second man."

"There was no second man."

"There were footprints in the garden."

"We ruled those out as yours," Hoffman said. "The initial impression was that they might have belonged to a third party, as they were the wrong size for you or Molly or the intruder we took into custody. But after some investigation, we found your gardening boots were a size too big."

"But what about the key safe? That no damage was done to gain entry. All our carers had been women, but those men used the key. The carer who took the key home that night, she must have given them the key."

"Inconsequential. We can't prove anything. There were no prints on the key, save from the carers."

I leaned back in the uncomfortable chair; I had known they wouldn't help, but Hoffman had seemed like a good person. He had to know there was another man involved but was choosing to ignore it to protect his record. I could feel my will to continue the discussion melting, Hoffman saw it too.

"Mr. Webb." He leaned forward. "I understand you've recently had a diagnosis of dementia." I rolled my eyes, making him pause. "Hear me out, this paranoia you're feeling. It's not real, it's caused by the sickness."

"You're a doctor now?" I barked, unable to control my frustration.

"My dad, he had the same, he… well, it's not important. No, Mr. Webb, I'm not a doctor, I'm just trying to help put you at ease. We caught the man who hurt your wife."

"Killed her," I said. "They beat her to death; she was five foot two and barely a hundred and twenty pounds and they beat her with a bat until she died."

"The man who killed your wife," Hoffman agreed. "There's nothing left for us to do, he's off the streets."

I thought about arguing but decided against it. It would be a pointless endeavour. Instead, I stood up, offered my hand to Hoffman and thanked him for his time.

*****

I didn't know what to do.

All my options had been exhausted. I had found the police report. I had confronted the police about the evidence of there being more than one perpetrator and had been ignored, or rather dismissed, as a mad old man. Sophie would never believe me, especially after letting slip I was seeing her mother again. She'd dismiss me as a mad old man as well. I had to stay away from her as much as possible. I couldn't talk to my doctor, he'd have me carted off to hospital faster than I could say my name.

"Art?" Molly whispered. She was resting on the sofa, watching me as I stood and looked out at the front garden. Mike had planted a hydrangea out there while I'd been out this morning.

"I'm tired. Tired of people only ever seeing the disease." I snorted a laugh. "I thought with an invisible illness you had to fight for people to acknowledge it, instead I wish no one knew and everyone seems to know."

"Calm down."

"I can't calm down," I snapped. "No one will take me seriously. They see me as an old boy losing his marbles."

"No one thinks that."

"You should have heard him." I finally sat down, my elbows resting on my knees. "Completely dismissed me."

"There are other options," Molly said after a long moment.

"What would those be? In case you haven't noticed, love, I'm no spring chicken. It's not like I could hunt him down myself."

"Art, don't snap."

"Sorry," I muttered. "I'm just worried."

"I know. I am as well, but panicking will not help. We need to be practical." She took a deep breath and stood up, leaving small flakes of grey skin and long brittle hairs on the sofa. "Perhaps I could help more."

"You're dead, honey."

"I am aware of that. Thank you, Arthur."

I bit my tongue. She only called me Arthur when she was mad at me. I went to try and smooth things over but a knock at the door stopped me. I glared at the front door and sighed; I didn't have time for this. But Molly had already vanished the moment I looked away. I would have to let her cool off before I could fix this. So, I got up carefully and went to the door. When I opened it, Doris stood on my doorstep smiling at me.

"Hello." She bustled past me, crock pot in hand, she laughed at my expression. "Oh, don't worry, I'm not here to prod at you, or make a fuss, just thought you could use some company and a meal."

"You are going to make me fat." I forced a smile as she set the pot down on the kitchen workstation. She was polite enough not to comment on the mess. "Can I get you some tea?" Doris gave me a long-suffering look, I gestured to the globe. "Help yourself." She did, heading over and pouring herself a generous helping of port.

"So, do they know what happened?" she came back to the kitchen. I shrugged.

"Not really. I think they think I'm a foolish old man."

"What do you mean?" Doris frowned.

"The police couldn't find anything to show that anyone broke in and the warden's comments…well, they seem to think I did it myself."

"Oh…" Doris stumbled with her words. "That sounds like nonsense to me. Where are your plates?"

"In one of the high up cupboards, the one by the window I think." I took the lid of the crock pot and the smell of lamb rose to meet me. She'd made a shepherd's pie. "There's a lot here."

Doris put the plates down next to the pot.

"I always find that if I cook a big portion, I don't have to make dinner every night, I can just reheat things."

"Clever girl." I looked around the bungalow, half expecting to see Molly glaring at me from the sofa. But there was no one else.

"Are you sure you're alright?" Doris heaped two portions onto the plates. "You seem awfully distracted."

"I'm fine, just a little jumpy I suppose."

"That's understandable." Doris didn't look convinced though, her brow furrowed and her eyes were dark. We took the plates into the living room and I turned the TV on, the sound down low. I took my first bite and like with breakfast the other day I suddenly realised just how hungry I was, I started shoveling food into my face.

"Are you sure you're alright?" Doris put her fork down. "I know, I know I said I wasn't here to fuss, but I can't help but notice that you seem different now to the day you moved in. You were so… well, more upbeat, more focused."

"Yes well—"

"I'm sorry, I know it's probably none of my business. But I know what it's like growing old and losing the person you thought you would spend the rest of your life with. It throws you for a loop in ways you don't expect. You should have seen me the first time I got a bill I had to pay myself, I didn't even know how to use the cheque book, Gerald did all the money stuff before. I was so lost."

"It must have been hard."

"It was and I can see your struggling, I can see how stressed you are, you always seem so preoccupied. Have you thought about maybe getting someone in to clean for you? They could keep your home nice; I can help with meals and-"

"I appreciate the thought," I interrupted.

"I'm sorry, I overstepped."

"Don't be sorry, you mean well and if you're noticing then I dread to think what it's doing to Sophie and I don't want her to worry."

"She's your daughter, she is going to worry no matter what you do." Doris picked up her fork again and started eating.

"I can't have her worrying, if she worries then she'll interfere and I can't have her doing that."

"Interfere? I don't think she would—"

"You don't understand." I was gripping my fork hard, the metal handle bit into my fingers. "She'll try to stop me and it's already so hard."

"Stop you from doing what?"

I let out a long breath and looked up at Doris. She was frowning hard at me, her eyes concerned and full of pity and worry. I'd said too much.

"Living by myself." My words came out flat and I didn't think Doris would believe me but her shoulders relaxed and she smiled. "I'm not well you see." I tapped the side of my head.

Doris frowned in confusion for a moment before her eyes widened in understanding.

"Sophie wasn't too keen on me moving in here on my own. I think she'll take any excuse to move me back in with her."

"Would that be so terrible?"

"It would." I stressed. "I don't want her or her children seeing me like that, I don't want their last memories of me being a frail, scared little old man. I want them to remember me as I am now."

"We don't get to choose how people remember us."

"I know, but I can try and keep the worst of it from them."

"They're family." Doris reached out and put her hand on my knee. "Don't push them away."

I didn't say anything, I went back to eating my dinner and watching the news. Doris didn't push the issue. We ate in companionable silence and Doris washed the dishes; she was a while in the kitchen probably cleaning the place if she was anything like Molly. I topped up her glass as a thank you. She left after an hour, again saying Max would be wanting his dinner. I watched her go, and smiled at her gentle reminder to lock my door before I went to bed.

"She seems nice." Molly said the moment the door closed. "She seems worried about you."

"Everyone's worried about me, that's the problem." I swallowed down the last of my whiskey before reaching for the bottle. "I'm sorry about before, love." I opened the bottle and poured a generous helping into my glass. "I didn't mean to upset you."

"I am dead." Molly sighed, watching me. "I know that and I've been thinking while you had your dinner, being dead has its advantages."

"It does?"

"Yes, I can go wherever I please."

"Handy."

"I can also talk to those who are stuck."

"There are others like you?"

Molly nodded. "Lots, poor things. They do nothing but watch the living. I could head back to the cottage and speak with any who might have seen what happened!" She slapped the arm of the sofa. "Why didn't I think of this before? They can tell me what they saw and I can tell you and you can go find the evidence."

"No one will listen to me."

"They won't if you keep drinking like that." Molly reached over and took my whiskey glass. "Right, I'm going to make you some tea, then I'll go chat." She walked into the kitchen.

I stood up and followed. I almost walked into an open cupboard. When had I left that open? What was the smell? I glanced at the bin. The lid was cracked open, rubbish piled up inside.

I watched Molly for a few moments. She wasn't facing me; she was focused on the task of making tea.

"I'm sorry for snapping." I watched her.

"What's that, Art?" Molly glanced over her shoulder at me.

"I said I'm sorry, love."

"I forgive you." She turned back to the kettle.

I walked over to her until I stood directly behind her. I was close enough to feel the chill coming off her and smell the strange mold smell coming from her skin. Leaning down, I kissed her behind the ear, as was my habit, and what was left of her hair tickled my face. She giggled, pushing me back.

"You're an old fool," she said. "I'm horrible now. You can't possibly want to kiss me."

"Don't care." I let her push me back a step. "I love you." I couldn't ignore how she looked like bones wrapped in a thin cotton dress. But despite this, she was still my Molly, and I loved her.

"Art, you might be happy to play around, but some of us have work to do."

"Fine, I'll behave." I turned to pick up the paper. It was yesterday's, but I hadn't read it yet.

"Art." Molly's voice was quivering.

My stomach clenched and ice shot down my back. "Molly?" I turned back to look at her.

"Someone's coming." She was shaking. "Someone who wants to hurt you. He knows you're after him!"

"Molly, he can't know. Hell, I don't even know myself."

"He does," Molly said. "He broke into the bungalow after you found the papers. He was looking for them. He's back! That man is going to stop you."

"Molly, shh, it's alright, no one's here, no one's coming." I reached out and closed my hand over hers. But I couldn't help the spike of anxiety in my gut.

Molly looked behind me. I went to turn to look, but Molly gasped and moved her hands from my shoulders up to cup the back of my head, stopping me from moving.

The blow came from behind and knocked me forward. As I fell, I reached out for the red cord by the wall. The cord snagged on my fingers- had I pulled it? I don't remember hitting the floor, but I saw Molly's slippered feet as I lay still. She screamed; heavy booted feet ran away. Molly crouched next to me, her face all I could see.

She stared directly at me through milk-white eyes. There was blood on her hands from my head. I couldn't feel anything. I tried to move, to get closer to her. I couldn't leave her alone again. But my body wouldn't respond. Molly crouched beside me, panicking, only inches away, and I couldn't reach her.

"I'm sorry." My head throbbed. "I should have been there. When they came, I should have been with you. I could have fought them." Even if I had failed, at least she wouldn't have had to die alone, beaten to death by strangers. "Molly." The world around me turned black.

Chapter Five

The hospital had a quiet chaos to it, a semi-silent hustle, as if the doctors and nurses were tiptoeing around. I sniffed and my nose filled with antiseptic stink. I'd woken up in the hospital two days ago with an anxious Sophie sitting by my bed. I didn't remember the paramedics arriving. I must have been unconscious and because the doctors couldn't say for sure how long I'd been unconscious, they kept me in.

After two days in the hospital, I was sick to death of the doctors and the smell. I was eager to go home.

"What is that smell?" I muttered.

"It's the gel they make you put on your hands," Sophie said. I huffed and pulled my shirt on slowly, trying to keep my movement slow and careful.

"It smells terrible. This whole place smells terrible."

Sophie rolled her eyes at me.

"It's a hospital, Dad, it's not meant to smell nice, it's meant to get you better. I don't know why you're getting dressed. You're not leaving till they discharge you."

"I've been here two days. I'm going home. Discharge or no discharge. It's a hospital, not a prison." I had to get out. Molly had been alone now for two days. Sophie walked over to me and brushed her fingers gently over my forehead. I winced.

"Bruise is looking nasty."

"The bruise showed up quickly. That means it isn't too bad. Everyone knows the faster a bruise comes out, the less serious it is."

"They wouldn't have given you an MRI scan if they didn't think it was bad," Sophie said. I snorted and winced as pain knifed through my head.

"I'm an old man." I took her hand. "They always double-check everything. They think I'm made of glass." Sophie squeezed my hand.

"Dad, stop trying to brush this off. You collapsed. People don't collapse for no reason; something is wrong."

"Probably just low blood sugar."

I had stopped arguing about the attack after the first day. I figured they would let me out sooner if I wasn't constantly telling them I'd been attacked when not one of them believed me. But I had been attacked. I'd felt the blow. Someone had hit me from behind, I was sure of it. But apparently there wasn't any kind of mark on the back of my head.

"Dad—" Sophie started, fortunately the doctor's arrival cut her off.

"Mrs. Ferguson, I'm glad to have caught you." The doctor glanced at me and nodded before turning back to Sophie. "I'm Dr. Stuart. Can you tell me how your dad has been lately?"

"I've been fine," I said, louder than I meant to. Dr. Stuart looked sheepish for a moment before turning to me.

"Sorry, Mr. Webb. How have you been?"

"Fine."

"He just moved out of his house," Sophie said. "We got a new place sorted, but it's still been a lot to deal with."

I rolled my eyes. "You guys did everything. All I did was go to a new house."

"It's still a stressful time," Dr. Stuart said.

"He moved out of the house he'd lived in for years with my mum," Sophie said.

"A big change." The doctor looked down at his notes. "Says here you recently had a break-in?"

"Possibly," I muttered.

"There's some debate about that," Sophie said. "Dad's not been well for some time, you see…" Her voice cracked as she spoke, and she coughed to clear it. The doctor looked at her for a long moment before glancing at his notes again.

"There's a mention in here of you talking to your wife? Is she here?"

"Mum died over a year ago."

"Hmm." Dr. Stuart flicked through the papers on his clipboard. "The ward nurses are a little confused about that, it says here you told them that someone broke in and attacked you and your wife."

"Dad?" Sophie said. I kept my eyes on Dr. Stuart, away from her.

"Well, Mr. Webb, the injury to your head is consistent with a fall, not a physical blow from a weapon." Dr. Stuart continued.

"Dad?" Sophie pressed. I looked at her this time.

"I had just had a fall, sweetheart; I was confused, that was all." Sophie didn't look convinced, neither did the doctor.

"Is this the first time you've fallen?" Dr. Stuart asked.

"Yes. Well, no. I had a few a couple of years back, but that was because of my hip. Since I got a new one, I haven't had any falls." The doctor let out a long breath.

"Well, your MRI scan came back as good as can be expected, given your condition. But I would like to refer you for further tests."

"I'm already going for tests."

"Yes, I can see from your records that your GP under advice from a Dr. Wakefield called through with a referral to neurology for tests. I think what I'll do..." He fidgeted with his papers again and jotted something down. "I'll expedite those tests and we'll see you again shortly after." With that, he turned and walked out of the cubicle. Sophie chased after him.

I stayed and buttoned up my shirt. I could hear her talking with the doctor outside.

"Doctor, can I ask you something?" Sophie said. I didn't hear the doctor's response, but it must have been an affirmative as she continued. "Did I do this?"

"How so?" the doctor asked.

I felt a lump form in my throat. Sophie thought she did this?

"I've been reading up about Dad's dementia, his GP said it was Lewy body dementia."

The doctor nodded.

"Stress makes it worse. Please tell me if I did this by making him move. He wanted to go back to the cottage but Mike and I, we pushed him to move somewhere we thought would be better. A place with more people, and activities - and wardens. But since the move, it's all been getting worse."

"Mrs. Ferguson-" the doctor started.

"Please, call me Sophie."

"Sophie, stress can increase the progression of all kinds of dementia. But I would be less concerned with the stress and more concerned with the fall. Physical trauma can, in some situations, speed the advancement of dementia."

"Oh." Sophie's voice was quiet.

"Not in all circumstances, but it is not uncommon. You understand the nature of your father's illness; it can only go one way. We can work to slow it, but it will not stop. You should prepare yourself for deterioration."

I lowered myself off the bed and glanced at the shelf where my shoes were sitting, trying not to listen to the conversation outside. Next to my shoes were two sheets of paper on which they'd had me draw shapes. I wasn't sure why, but apparently it was something to do with my brain. It tempted me to write something unkind on them but thought better of it.

"Dad." Sophie sounded strained as she came back in. I turned to her, and she walked up and wrapped her arms around me. "I'm so sorry."

"Don't be daft, love." I patted her arm. "Doctors, they don't know everything. I feel perfectly fine." I pushed Sophie back a little so I could see her face. Her eyes were red-rimmed and wet. "I like the bungalow; I'm glad I went there. I have new friends now, Doris, from next door." I forced a smile. "I'm glad you talked me into the move. You and Mike were right; the cottage wasn't doing me any good. I don't want you blaming yourself for what's happened; it's just rotten luck and my carelessness."

"But-"

"No buts, now come and help me with my laces. My back's aching and I want to go home now."

The grandkids were in the car. It surprised me at Sophie leaving them in there for so long, but I said nothing. Instead, I spent the drive home listening to them bicker and smiling at their arguments. We reached the bungalow, and when I walked in it was immediately apparent that Sophie had come in and cleaned while I was in the hospital. The kids turned on the television and I looked around the living room and kitchen for Molly.

"You had cups everywhere," Sophie said. "Do you ever finish a cup of tea?"

"I have occasionally finished one," I said. Sophie took a deep breath and didn't meet my eyes.

"You are eating at the centre a lot?"

"A fair bit, yes," I lied. "Doris also made a few meals for me. Why?"

"Never mind," Sophie said. "I'll just know to get less shopping in." I glanced at the bin. Lifting the lid, it was full of unopened food: a loaf of bread, a punnet of eggs.

"Sorry to be so wasteful," I said. "I've been so busy."

"I'm just making sure you're eating all your veggies." Sophie sounded strained; her voice choked.

"You alright love?" I asked.

"It's just a cough. The boys bring every germ in existence home from school. I've always got a bit of something," she said. "How about we go out for lunch? You've not got anything in now."

"Sounds good. How about the little café on the dunes?"

"Lovely," Sophie said. "I just want to nip to the toilet."

"I'll get the boys out to the car," I said, turning away. "Come on, lads, we're off out for lunch!"

"But it's only half 10!" Simon said.

"We're going for a walk first," I said. "Come on, we'll wait for Mum in the car."

Oscar raced out of the bungalow and stood bouncing by the car, encouraging us to come on. I settled the boys in then headed back inside to get my wallet. Walking past the bathroom, I heard Sophie talking.

"Worse… not eating. Nothing's been opened, everything's gone bad. I'm worried."

I flinched at her words.

"There were cups all over the bungalow. I swear it's like he starts making a drink, then loses track. There was dirty laundry in one of the kitchen cupboards and…." She stopped. "Alright, alright. Look, we're going out for lunch. I'll talk to you when I get back. Love you too."

I shuffled back out to the car and made it to the front door when the toilet flushed and the bathroom door opened.

"All good?" Sophie asked me.

"Just got the wallet. Shouldn't need a coat. It's pretty warm today."

"It'll be breezy on the dunes."

"Last time I checked, young lady," I said, "I was your dad; don't you be nagging me."

"Alright." Sophie kissed my cheek. "But if you get cold, don't blame me."

The boys talked while we drove the short distance to the dunes; what they'd been playing at school, who was in what gang and who had the highest score on a video game. By the time Sophie parked the car I did not know what they were talking about, all this nonsense about points for this coloured ball and different points for another colour. I swear kids were getting odd as time went on.

We let them out of the car and watched as they tore off across the dunes. Sophie called out to them not to go near the water or too far ahead, but the boys either didn't hear or, more likely, ignored her. I laughed as Sophie huffed and fussed at them, remembering when Molly had done the same thing with Sophie and her brother. She'd been so worried about them getting too near to the water.

"I'm just being careful," Sophie said, catching me smiling.

"The ocean won't jump up and grab them," I said.

"Yes, well." Sophie snorted. "I am aware, but I know also that the boys have no idea of their own mortality and will charge into the water blindfolded if it was up to them."

"Your mum had the same fear. Kids never appreciate how dangerous the world is. I wish I could remember what that felt like."

"Yeah," Sophie said. "Me too." She smiled suddenly. "Do you remember when we used to bring Bruno up here?"

"That damn dog." I chuckled at her. "He had a death wish, constantly dragging you close to the water. I thought your mum was going to kill him." I remembered how flustered Molly would get every time the overgrown puppy would tug at Sophie. I tried to stop her taking his lead but she'd cry every time until I'd relent.

"She never let me take his lead after the visit to Cromer," Sophie laughed. Molly had eventually put her foot down when Bruno had actually gotten Sophie into the sea.

"No, that became my job," I said. "Damn dog nearly dislocated my shoulder a few times."

"I miss Bruno," Sophie said. "He was amazing."

"He was as dumb as mud, but yes, he was a wonderful dog." I nodded.

"Mum told me she made you take him to the vet on your own in the end. She couldn't bear to see it when they put him down." Bruno had been old, his life was painful, he struggled to get to his feet, to the point where he couldn't make it outside to pee. Letting him go had been a kindness.

"Your mother was soft-hearted."

"Sometimes being soft-hearted isn't always the right thing, though. Bruno would have suffered longer if you hadn't let them put him down and he'd have died on his own if you hadn't gone with him."

"Sometimes things that seem awful are the right thing." I thought about my decision to put myself in a home and not tell Sophie where I was. It would be cruel to her, but in the long run, it was the right thing to do. I sniffed and made a mental note to write her a letter. I couldn't just disappear on her. Hopefully she would understand and maybe one day, she would forgive me.

"It's been so long since I've been here," Sophie said, watching the boys playing a way ahead.

"Yes," I said. "I'm glad we came down today. I want to remember this place."

"Dad?" Sophie said. I swallowed.

"I'm afraid," I said, forcing the words out. "I don't want to forget. I'm trying so hard not to, but it doesn't seem to work." I took a deep breath. "I wasn't feeling great today when I woke up, so I'm glad we came here. I feel better and I think if I'm feeling good there's a better chance I'll remember this place, this day, with you and the boys." Sophie sniffed, and I caught her wiping a few tears away.

"Dad," she managed.

"Get those boys a dog," I blurted. "All boys need a dog to grow up with. A Labrador I think."

"Like Bruno?" Sophie said, and I nodded. "I'll talk to Mike," she said. The cheer drained from her face. "Dad, in the graveyard when you said you were seeing Mum." I felt the cold wash over me and from Sophie's expression, it showed on my face. I regretted telling her about seeing Molly. It was a stupid thing to do. She had to hear something to convince her I was okay.

"I know it can't be real, but there's a part of me that wanted it to be," I said. "I know the difference between what's real and what isn't." I glanced behind us; Molly stood in the dunes a little way back. She raised a withered arm in greeting.

"I know, Dad," Sophie said. Molly smiled at me, her dead skin stretching horribly over bones. It was nightmarish to see her like that, more so because of the genuine love in her eyes. I took Sophie's hand and squeezed tightly as she glanced to where Molly stood and saw nothing.

*****

Sophie dropped me off at the gate and drove away, her eyes red from unshed tears. I walked up the hill towards the bungalow and was surprised to meet Doris coming the other way.

"Your daughter called me," she said by way of greeting.

Why was Sophie calling Doris? How did she even know Doris' phone number?

"I gave her my number when I saw her moving your furniture in, she seemed worried so I thought it might be reassuring for her to be able to get hold of a neighbour if she couldn't get hold of you."

"What did she want? When did she call you? Is something wrong?" I reached into my pocket to see if Sophie had tried to call me. I had no missed calls.

"Only a moment ago, she's worried about you, thinks you could use a friend. So, I have cleared my calendar for the day, and you and I are going to have some fun."

"I appreciate the offer, but I just got back from the hospital-"

"Yes, you fell." Doris' smile faded. "I've had a few falls and they always leave me feeling sorry for myself. So, you don't get to argue, we're going to cheer you up."

I sighed.

"Oh, don't look so grumpy. We're only going up to the Hall." Doris took my arm and marched me up towards the community hall. I glanced at the bungalow as we went passed, half expecting to see Molly in the window, but she wasn't there. "They're showing Casablanca at the little cinema this afternoon."

The Hall had a quiet buzz about it when we entered. The main hall had a few tables set up, and most were occupied by what looked like board games. I noticed a sign explaining there was a bar down the corridor, the cinema room upstairs and the game room behind us.

"Perfect timing." Doris pulled me into the bar and I couldn't help the little bubble of amusement that popped in my chest. Doris was fun and with everything going on I couldn't remember the last time I'd been genuinely charmed by anyone.

I wondered at my reaction to Doris' playfulness as she encouraged me over to the bar. I had always expected to feel guilt at spending time with another woman, maybe the lack of guilt was because Doris wasn't a replacement for Molly, she was just good company, a friend?

"What can I get you?" the lady behind the bar asked. I froze for a moment. I had no idea what Doris would want to drink, I knew she liked putting brandy in her cakes, but she'd had port with dinner.

"Um I'll have a whisky," I said, "and...um."

"Make that two whisky's." Doris finished the order for me. I paid for the drinks and we sat at a table.

"Thank you, Arthur." She lifted her glass to me.

"I didn't know if you wanted soda or cola or…"

"Don't be silly, neat is exactly how whisky should be drunk." Doris knocked the drink back smoother than any man I had ever seen. I smiled at her and raised my glass in a salute.

"Then, dear lady, let me join you." I knocked back the whisky and coughed as it hit the back of my throat; it had been a long time since I drank like that.

"Susan?" Doris called.

"Yes?" the lady at the bar called back.

"Could you give me a tab this evening?"

"Of course, Doris." Susan smiled. "You stay put I'll bring two more over for you."

"Susan is very kind," Doris said to me. "Her daughter just went off to university to study Chemistry, isn't that fancy."

"Very, must be a clever girl." I glanced at the clock; it was half past one.

"She's a sweet girl, she helps out her mum in the summer, runs some of the game nights. Your daughter, what does she do?"

Susan came and put two more drinks on the table. I watched as Doris lifted her glass and sipped. I did the same.

"Sophie looks after her two boys at home at the moment, but she's been talking about getting back into work now that they're a bit older. She used to work as a Human Resources manager."

"That sounds interesting."

"She loved it. It's one of the reasons I don't want to move in with them again. It would stop her going back to work if she suddenly had me to look after."

"But you could help her, you could look after your grandkids."

"No, I can't. I'm sick remember." I tapped the side of my head as I had before. "It's only going to get worse. What if I was looking after the boys and something happened? Not to mention I don't want my grandkids seeing me like that." I looked at the clock again, I could see it clearly but for some reason I couldn't tell what time it was.

"You seem to be in a bit of a hurry."

"What?"

"You keep looking at the clock? Did you have plans this afternoon?"

"Oh…" I stopped. Doris was a friend and, as she had said when we had dinner together, she understood what it was like to lose someone you thought you'd spend the rest of your life with, maybe she'd understand what I was doing? I looked down, staring at my drink while I thought.

"Arthur," Doris said, I looked up. "Something's wrong, isn't it?"

"No." I swallowed the lump in my throat.

"You're a terrible liar." Doris leaned back in her seat. "Most men are."

"I'm not…" I trailed off. "You wouldn't believe me if I told you."

"I might." Doris frowned. "Is this what you were talking about the night you had your fall? You said Sophie would stop you and then gave me a line about living on your own."

"Saw through that huh?"

"You're a bad liar."

"Fair." I could feel sweat break out across my back. "Ok. But…" I stopped struggling to think of a way to word things without making Doris think I was mad. Now that I knew she was speaking to Sophie, I had to be careful. I could give her another story, but she'd see right through it. So perhaps the truth but not all of it.

"Arthur, you're worrying me."

"Sorry. Alright, there is something. I've not told you everything about Molly, and how she died."

"I assumed she was sick."

"No. She wasn't sick. Men broke into our home when I was in hospital getting my hip replaced. They robbed us and they killed my Molly."

"Oh God!" Doris put her hand over her mouth.

"They attacked her in her bed, she managed to crawl out of the bed and get to the stairs but… Sophie found her the next morning at the bottom of the stairs."

"Oh God Arthur, I'm so sorry. Did the police get the men who did it?"

"One of them."

"What about-"

"They're not interested in the second one. They pretend he doesn't exist. I'm trying to find him myself."

"But how?"

"I've been doing some investigating. Before I went into hospital my hip was in a bad way, I couldn't get about much and we had some carers they'd come in and help me have a wash. They did some of the heavy lifting jobs that Molly couldn't do on her own. They had a key to the cottage, a key that went missing."

"Oh?"

"The police couldn't find signs of forced entry the night Molly was killed."

"You think the carers were involved?"

"I do. I can't prove it yet, but I'm going to keep trying. Molly can't rest, you see, not until I find who killed her, and Sophie, God bless her, she doesn't believe me, she thinks I'm just a sick old man. But I know I'm right, and I know that the person who killed Molly knows as well."

"What!"

"The break in at the bungalow, that was them trying to figure out what I know. The fall I had, I didn't bloody fall, they came and attacked me. Doctors are covering it up, because it's easier to say I'm an old man with dementia than admit the truth."

"The truth?"

"That my wife was murdered and the killer is still out there, watching me hunt him down."

Doris didn't say anything. She stared at me hard for a long moment before finishing her drink. Her hand was shaking when she put her glass down.

"Well." She stood up. "I can't imagine what you're going through. But just for an afternoon I think it would be a good idea if you took it easy. Come on finish your drink, they're showing Casablanca upstairs at 2pm. While it's a bit corny, I think we should watch it. Take your mind off things." Doris was speaking very quickly her words running together.

"Corny? How dare you." I smiled to let her know I was joking.

"Fine it's a timeless classic. Now come on, I need to use the little girl's room and I plum forgot I need to call my son, he was supposed to be coming over this afternoon, he'll be wondering where I am, so we need to get a wiggle on."

"Damn right a timeless classic." I followed Doris out of the bar and upstairs.

Chapter Six

Molly walked out of the kitchen as I finished taking off my shoes. She was wearing a pale blue dress; the skirt was long and billowed as she walked. It did little to mask her greying skin, skeletally thin legs and the decay eating away at her. Her perfume did nothing to hide the smell hanging over her. I felt bile rise in my throat again. So little of who she had been remained. She didn't look like my Molly anymore. Even her eyes, now cloudy and white, seemed blank. She was a walking corpse.

"Where have you been!" She frowned at me. I noticed that some of her teeth were missing. "I've been waiting and waiting." She pursed her lips pulling her skin tight. Her left cheek tore a little under the strain. I had let this happen to her. She was like this because of me. I had failed her repeatedly.

"Molly." I stepped forward, my arms outstretched.

"Please don't." She put up her hand, stopping me. "I can't, not when I'm like this."

"But I don't—"

"You didn't come home after seeing Sophie."

"No dear, I'm sorry I got waylaid. I couldn't get away without making people worry and the more they worry-"

"Yes, I know." Molly watched me, her panicked expression relaxing slowly. "I'm sorry I didn't mean to snap. But I was so eager for you to come home, I have some marvellous news."

"Oh?"

"I can show you where he is." She grinned, her skin stretching garishly over her cheekbones. I jolted back as if she had burned me.

"What? You know who he is?" Her eyes looked distant, as if she was looking at something not in this room.

"I do. I don't know his name. I can show you where he is, though."

"How did you find him?"

"I spoke to the ones hanging around the cottage. It took a while to get them to speak to me. But they did. Come on, now!"

"Molly, please." I stepped forward and wrapped my arms around her. She put her hands on my chest and pushed back.

"Art. I need you to do this for me." She looked up, tears staining her cheeks. "I couldn't bear to be here without you."

"But I would never leave you."

"You won't have a choice. That's why I need you to do this for me now." She turned away from me, gliding as if she had never had arthritis in her knees, something that had plagued the last few years of her life. I watched as she walked towards the door, repeating her words in my mind as I followed her. Would I leave her? I didn't want to. But what if she was right? What if I had no choice? What would happen when I died? What if I moved on? She'd be here alone. I couldn't do that to her.

"Okay, Molly," I said with a deep breath. "What do I need to do?"

"Follow me." She walked to the front door

She walked on silent feet, out into the garden and down the path. I followed without thinking; I got to the end of the path before I realised, I had no shoes on, no stick and no coat. Molly kept walking.

"Wait." I glanced around to make sure no one had heard, knowing full well no one else could see my Molly. Fortunately, it was late, and no one else was outside. Molly didn't stop. I watched as she kept walking. The doctors would think I was mad, chasing my long-dead wife down the street. But as I watched her walk away from me, my chest grew tight. The thought of leaving her alone, letting her walk away from me now when I had failed her so badly before. I couldn't let her keep suffering because I wasn't there when she needed me. I could be there for her now. She needed me now. I kept walking. I had survived worse than a bit of cold and a lack of shoes.

I made it a few more feet down the road before I stopped again. This was painful, and I was even slower than normal. I would be more help if I could walk better. I turned and looked back at the bungalows behind me.

They were all exactly the same.

I knew Mike had put a plant in my front garden, something to help me remember, which was mine. Molly had loved the rhododendron we'd had back at the cottage. Mike must have put one in. But none of these gardens had a rhododendron.

"Arthur, come on. Please." Molly's voice was desperate. I turned back to face her and started walking again.

We walked out of the retirement community and onto the main road. Molly stopped and looked hard at me.

"You need to call a taxi. You won't make it there without one." There was a taxi rank on the edge of the town centre. I could walk that far.

I reconsidered that thought after a little over ten minutes. Walking in your socks is a lot harder than walking in shoes. The ground is much colder and harder than you think it is. My bones were not as strong as the concrete, and it wasn't long before I started limping, then I slowed and started yearning to sit down.

"Call a taxi," Molly told me, her voice impatient.

"Left the phone at home, besides can't work the damn tiny thing," I muttered, looking around at the quiet suburban street. "The buttons are the size of ants."

"Please, Art." Molly sniffed. I looked at her; the expression of desperation on her face gave me the strength to speed up again.

"Ok girl, I'm coming." I gritted my teeth against the cold and pain working its way up from the soles of my feet.

I was limping badly by the time I reached the taxi rank.

When I opened the door, I fell into the passenger seat. I sat for a moment, catching my breath and trying to ignore the pain in my feet and legs. I noticed Molly in the back seat, sitting quietly, staring at me in the rear-view mirror.

"You ok, old timer?" The taxi driver watched me carefully. I forced a smile.

"Hello, sorry about that. It's been a long night," I said. The driver glanced at my feet, noting the lack of shoes.

"It's my grandson's stag night, things got out of hand." I was surprised at my ability to think of a lie so quickly.

"Tell him to go to Abbey Road." Molly leaned forward from the back seat. The taxi driver did not hear her.

"Can you take me to Abbey Road?" I said. The driver cracked a smile and nodded.

"Yeah, no problems, mate. My boy had his stag night last month, was married a few days later, they had to use makeup to cover up the black eye he 'somehow' got." The driver laughed. "Not to mention the tattoo."

He continued to laugh as we pulled out into traffic. I fidgeted in the seat, pulling the seatbelt on for something to do. I watched the town slip past. I had no idea where Abbey Road was; I'd never heard of it. I looked in the rear-view mirror and saw Molly staring out of the window. Her expression was serious, but calm.

"You ok? You expecting company?"

"What? No."

"Just that you keep looking in the rear-view mirror." I looked into the mirror again. Molly was staring at me. She nodded and smiled; we were going in the right direction.

"I'm ok, just tired."

"Ok. As long as you're sure." The driver did not sound convinced. Fortunately, Abbey Road wasn't far. In less than fifteen minutes, Molly leant forward and put her hand on my shoulder.

"Tell him to stop on the left." Her breath tickled my ear, and I held my breath against the stench.

"Stop here please, on the left." My mouth was dry. We pulled over slowly.

"That's..." The driver started leaning forward to fidget with the meter. I pulled a twenty-pound note out of my wallet and handed it to him.

"Keep the change." I stepped out of the car.

"You sure?" the driver called as I shut the door and started walking down the path.

The street was broken, the paving slabs cracked and uneven. I watched where I put my feet, especially when I spotted a torn black bin bag spilling its contents into the road. The buildings here were tall and old looking, tower blocks housing hundreds of people. Graffiti covered the walls and, for a moment, I wondered how the vandals had scrawled profanity up so high.

"Why here, Molly?" I turned when the taxi pulled away.

"This is where he is." Molly stepped up beside me.

"Here?" My head was fuzzy, like I had gone too long without proper rest despite spending the last few days in the hospital. I was struggling to make any sense out of what I was doing. I had followed my wife, who had died over a year ago, to a place I had never been because she told me she could show me her killer. A killer no one else thought existed. I had left without shoes, coats or my stick. I was defenceless. My chest suddenly clenched tight, and sweat broke out across my face. I did not know where I was, and no way to get home. I didn't even know my proper address beyond number twenty-four. What was I doing?

"Him," Molly said.

"Molly, we have to go back," I reached for her, taking one of her hands in both of mine. But she pulled away.

"No, Art." Her footsteps on the pavement left little dried clumps of skin behind, bone shone through her heel. She was getting worse so quickly. I watched her shoulders as she walked, leading me to the one who had killed her.

Briefly, I wondered what the hell I would do once I reached him. I was no slouch. Days in the RAF and then working around heavy machines after I was discharged had kept me robust enough, but that was decades ago. These days I wouldn't stand a chance against anyone. But perhaps I could watch him, wait for him to make a mistake? Or maybe I could approach him, get him talking? I shook my head. This wasn't an action film, and I wasn't a movie spy. What the hell was I going to do?

"Hey." A heavy hand landed on my shoulder. "You ok, wait, Mr. Webb, is that you?"

"Perfectly fine." I drew myself up as much as I could. I frowned, recognising the warden, James.

"What are you doing here? Who are you talking to?"

"No one." I felt my face heat as I blushed.

"Where are your shoes?" He put the carrier bag he was holding down. "Do you know where you are?"

"Actually—" I started. But my confusion must have been apparent.

"Come and sit down." He led me towards a tower block with grey concrete steps. "Do you remember how you got here?"

"I do," I snapped.

"Do you know where your shoes are? Are you meeting someone?"

I shook my head.

"Is there anyone I can call? Your daughter maybe?" James asked.

I had visions of Sophie coming to get me and shook my head hard.

"No," I said. "I'll just get a taxi."

"Art." Molly was suddenly next to me. "Art, you can't leave."

"You want me to call you a taxi? Do you have any money?"

I didn't answer. I was too busy staring at Molly.

"You've found him," she hissed. "It's him! He's the one who killed me!"

*****

The taxi pulled up to the hospital, and I saw Sophie waiting by the door.

"Dad!" Sophie sounded so genuinely relieved as I stepped out of the taxi, the embarrassment I felt quickly turned to shame. "Are you all right?"

Her hands closed on my shoulders briefly before pulling me into a hug. Her arms for all that they were shaking felt strong around me, larger than they should, and it suddenly hit me how frail I must seem to her. No longer her powerful father, who could carry her on his shoulders. Now I was a foolish, frail old man, nothing but a nuisance, a cause of worry and stress.

"He's fine, Miss," James said.

"Then why bring me here?" I muttered.

"Where are your shoes?" Sophie said, ignoring James for a moment. I said nothing.

"Don't fret miss, we see this a lot here. It's rarely anything to be concerned about. Probably just a mix-up with the medication. If you want to talk to the office, we can arrange for Mr. Webb to have medication prompts?"

"Sorry, what?" Sophie finally seemed to notice James. "Oh, I'm sorry, you must be James. Thank you for calling me."

"No trouble," James said. "I was just saying that confusion like this isn't always a sign that-"

"I'm losing my mind."

"Dad, don't say that," Sophie snapped. "It's an illness, that's all, and maybe James is right. Maybe we should look at your medication." She flushed a deep red. "I can't believe I didn't check it."

"I'm not a child, I can take my own damn pills."

"I know." Sophie's tone changed, going very soft, the voice she used when the kids were being unreasonable.

I took a deep breath; my heart was hammering in my chest. The taxi ride had been difficult. Sitting in the back next to the person Molly claimed killed her and keeping quiet was difficult. I looked at him hard, had he really been the one to kill my Molly? I could hardly believe it, but she sounded so sure. He had seemed so genuine. But then he had basically admitted to me that he did drugs, or at least his friends did. That didn't make him a murderer though. But the police said the person who had killed Molly had been trying to rob us because they owed money to dangerous people. Maybe James did too? He certainly didn't look like he had two pennies to rub together. But he helped me? He certainly didn't seem the type to hurt anyone.

"Sorry, love." I tried to sound calm, to not betray my confusion.

"It's all right, Dad." Sophie's strained smile did not reach her eyes. "Let's go inside. I'll just pay the taxi and meet you inside."

I headed into the hospital while Sophie paid for the taxi and thanked James again.

"I'm just going to use the bathroom," I said as Sophie came inside.

"Be careful," Sophie called after me.

I bit my tongue and kept walking.

"Stupid old man," I hissed at myself. Of course, people would see me wandering the streets, talking to myself and think I was sick. Add to that the worries Sophie already had, and I was asking for trouble. I had to be more careful. I couldn't let her stop me now, not when I was so close.

But close to what? I knew who he was, but what could I do about it? I didn't have any proof and I was rapidly running out of time to do anything. Molly was falling apart before my eyes. My daughter was looking at me with more worry and concern each day. It was only a matter of time before Sophie did something. If I lost my independence, Molly was lost forever. I had to act, and I had to act fast, but I had to be careful.

"Arthur." Molly was behind me as soon as the door closed and I was alone.

"Molly. Where did you go?"

"I couldn't bear to be in the taxi with him. I didn't mean to leave you, but I just couldn't." Tears fell down her face.

"Love," I said softly. "Are you sure it was him?"

Molly's expression hardened, her eyebrows coming down and her mouth tightening.

"Absolutely."

"Really?"

"You doubt me? Arthur the man killed me, he's not someone I'm likely to forget."

"But he's Doris' lad, he's the one who fixed our sink before I got my hip sorted, he just… doesn't seem the type."

Molly let out an exasperated huff.

"Arthur, killers don't wear badges." She fidgeted for a moment as if struggling with her words. "Besides, I don't think they came in with the intention to kill me."

"Sweetheart." I reached out to her to pull her close but she held up a hand.

"I don't remember all of it, I'll admit. But I do remember him, how surprised he was, how angry he was that I was there. He lashed out in a fit of temper and panic because I saw who he was and I knew him." She was crying again. "Please Art, it was him."

"Don't fret, old girl." I brushed the tears away with my thumb. Her skin fell apart like tissue paper under my touch, gleaming bone showed through. I wrapped my arms around her. She felt thin and frail under my grip. "I'm so sorry."

"Sorry?" Molly said. "But you've found him, you've almost done it!"

"But what now? We know who he is, but how do we prove it? No one will listen to me. I'm a mad old man."

"You're not mad." Molly tightened her grip on me. Her arms felt like bars against my back. "You're right. We're running out of time. We might have to do something drastic."

"Drastic?" My voice broke.

"Calm down. You're panicking and you're no good to me if you're in a fright."

"Sorry, love," I managed around the lump in my throat. The door opened and Sophie came in.

"Dad, you ok?"

I nodded and followed her to the waiting area.

"Sorry, love," I said as we sat down to wait.

"Don't apologise, Dad. It's not your fault."

"I'm a foolish old man."

"No, I knew you were getting worse and not once did I ask about your pills."

"I'm a grown man. You shouldn't have to ask me about my damned pills."

"But you're not taking them, are you?" Sophie said.

I shook my head.

"Why?"

"It wasn't intentional. I just sort of stopped."

"Dad." Sophie took a deep breath. "Promise me you'll start taking the medicine."

"All right," I said. "I will. I promise. Can we just go home?"

"We need to get you checked. They'll probably keep you in overnight just to be careful." Sophie shook her head. "But I've arranged for the wardens to make morning calls to you. They'll remind you to take the pills."

"I can manage—" I started, but Sophie stopped me.

"It's just a telephone call. They won't come around, or watch you take the pills. It's just a gentle reminder in case you forget. James said he does the same thing for his mum."

"All right. I can live with that."

*****

I woke to the smell of antiseptic, the particular antiseptic that I only ever came across in my local hospital. I disliked that I was so familiar with it that the smell alone was enough to tell me where I was. The doctors had insisted that I stay overnight for observation.

"Next week?" Sophie shouted, her sudden outburst making me twitch. She sounded so much like Molly. I opened my eyes and looked at her. She stood at the end of my bed, tiny but fierce. Dr. Stuart took a step back from her, looking down at his clipboard, not making eye contact.

"I can't discharge him into his own care," Dr. Stuart said. "This is his second admission in less than 48 hours; the medication is no longer controlling the hallucinations."

"Yes, but—" Sophie started.

"The CT Scan shows a marked deterioration from his early scans."

"He won't be on his own. He lives in a retirement community. There are wardens who have agreed to monitor him. He's moving in with me. We just need a little time to get it sorted."

I frowned. When was that decided? I coughed to get their attention.

"I only just moved out a few days ago?" I said.

Sophie looked at me, and Dr. Stuart backed away.

"Dad, you're awake."

"I'm moving again?" My voice came out quiet and shaking. Sophie glanced at the retreating doctor before looking back at me and speaking quietly.

"They won't discharge you otherwise. It was either move in with me with a specialist carer on the books or..." she trailed off.

"Stay here." I sighed. "Or a home."

"I thought it was the lesser of the evils." She swallowed, blinking rapidly. "We just need a day or so to get things sorted, but the doctors won't let you go home till then. They want you to stay here."

"And then they moan about overfilled hospitals."

"Dad, I know you don't want to live with us, but I promise it won't be bad. We're already getting the extension tidied up with new carpets and Mike's finishing the wiring this weekend. It will be your own place, just attached to us. Like a neighbour." She smiled, but it was wobbly. "The kids will know not to come in and pester you all the time, and you can come and go as you please." She paused and seemed to rethink that. "Well, sort of. Either way, I'll be there, and I can take you anywhere you want to go."

"Sophie. Don't say that."

She frowned at me.

"You make it sound like I hate you and I don't. You know I don't. I just don't want to be in the way; you've got enough to worry about with Mike and the kids. You don't need a pain in the arse old man clogging up the place."

"Don't exaggerate." Sophie sniffed, but her smile was brighter now. "I know you don't want to give up your freedom, your independence. I wouldn't want to either. You won't have to give up freedom if you live with us. As much as we can, we will keep your independence."

"I don't want to be a bother," I said again, not wanting to say that I didn't want her to watch me decline. I didn't want her to have to watch me die. "You're young. You deserve to live your life with your family."

"What do you think you are if not my family? You are our family, Dad; we want you with us."

I sighed. It didn't matter what Sophie said, nothing would change how this felt. A guest bedroom in my daughter's house. Even if it was an extension.

"Sophie."

"There aren't a lot of options now. This is the best one, I promise." She looked at me hard, and I had to work not to flinch. Her expression was strained, almost as if she was trying desperately to see her dad in my face and not finding him.

"All right sweetheart," I gave in. "Just don't be touching the globe. It's delicate."

"Don't worry, we prefer wine."

"Beer actually," Mike walked in. My son-in-law smiled at me. "You can keep your lighter fluid booze, old man. Give me a cold pint and I'm happy."

"I could tolerate a bitter, I suppose." I forced a smile back at him. "Or a stout."

"I'll fill the fridge." Mike put his arm around Sophie. "Hun, look what I found." He held out a small white box, about the size of a beeper, and Sophie took it, looking as confused as I felt.

"What is it?" she said.

"It's a personal alarm." Mike grinned. "I was talking to that warden who's taken a shine to your dad, and they said a few of the chaps have them. They're like the alarms in the bungalows, but portable."

Sophie smiled widely and leant in to give Mike a quick kiss on the cheek.

"Stay right there," she handed him the alarm back and darted out.

"Well," Mike said. "I'll bring her more alarms if it gets me kisses." I chuckled. Sophie came back in, all but dragging the poor doctor behind her. She took the alarm from Mike and shoved it at Dr. Stuart.

"What if he had this?"

"Well," Dr. Stuart said.

"The nurse is bringing in a walking frame," Mike said.

"A zimmer frame!" I couldn't stop myself. "Just put me out of my misery now."

"If it means you can come home, then a frame is a minor concession," Sophie said.

"But I'll look old."

"Drinking whisky makes you look old," Mike said. I gave him a hard look, and he grinned. "How about we put go faster stripes on the frame? Like race cars or your warplanes?" I couldn't help but snort at the remark.

"Flames," I said. "Paint it black and put flames on it, and I'll think about it."

"There, we've got an arrangement with the wardens in place, an alarm and a walking frame and it's only for a day or two till we can get things sorted at home," Sophie said firmly to Dr. Stuart. Dr. Stuart sighed.

"If you sign the release papers confirming I've advised you of the risks, then ok."

It didn't take long for Sophie and Mike to get the papers signed. While Sophie softly badgered and harassed the hospital staff, Mike helped me to dress.

"I'm not getting in the wheelchair."

"We'll get out a hell of a lot faster if you do," Mike said. "Plus, I want to see you pop a wheelie."

"No." I buttoned up my shirt with some difficulty. "I don't care if it does warp speed. I'm not getting in the chair." Mike leant in closer to me and dropped his voice a bit.

"I don't know if you noticed, but they don't want to let you out of here," he whispered. "Sophie's had to argue back and forth for the last two hours. They're worried about your mental capacity and your mobility. The more we show cooperation, the more likely it is we'll all walk or roll out of here today."

"She's been pressing that hard?"

"She was on the phone with them at eight o'clock this morning. She thinks you being here will make you sicker. She knows how much you hate it, how agitated it's making you."

I sighed. Sophie had put a lot of effort into getting me out of the hospital, knowing how much I hated it here. I wouldn't act like a spoilt child and undo her hard work.

"All right." I got into the chair. "But no wheelies."

"Spoilsport." Mike turned me around. He started to push me out of the ward before running back to grab my bag. Dropping my bag onto my lap, he finally got me out of the ward. "Right, that's hurdle one." He started walking faster.

"You lunatic," I snorted when he started jogging. "You'll kill us both."

"Freedom!"

"You're not amusing." I couldn't help chuckling. Thankfully, Mike slowed to a normal pace.

"Would have been even better if you'd let me do a wheelie."

"Mike!" Sophie was jogging after us. "Do not run with my dad!"

"He's my dad now! You'll never catch us, copper."

"This isn't a joking matter," Sophie said, but when I glanced at her, she was smiling. "What if they saw you? I've been trying to convince them we're good, responsible people and you mess about."

"Sorry, love. Couldn't resist."

"I bet you couldn't," Sophie said. We made it out to the car park, and I smiled as Sophie visibly relaxed. "Something funny, Dad?" Sophie said as Mike helped me up out of the damned wheelchair and I got into the car.

"Just that you hate that place more than I do." I watched as Mike took the wheelchair back to the hospital.

"Yeah, well," Sophie got into the car. "It's where Mum was taken. I hate the smell of the place; it reminds me of..." she trailed off. Mike got back to the car and, sensing the atmosphere, didn't speak as Sophie drove out of the car park and onto the main road.

The hospital wasn't far from the village, less than a ten-minute drive. Mike helped me get the damned walking frame out of the car and to ease the worried look Sophie was giving me, I used it to get up the path a little way. Sophie's worried look didn't fade; I wasn't the only one to notice.

"Hun, how about I stay the night here, with your dad," Mike blurted.

"What?" I asked.

"I don't mean to invite myself, but I'm sure it would make Sophie feel better. How about it?" he asked me. "We can watch a bit of television, have a few drinks. I know you've got more than whisky in that globe."

"Did Molly tell you everything? All my secrets?"

"Pretty much. I'll kip on the sofa, and you can come and get me in the morning, hun, I'm on breakfast shift so it'll be a bit early but—"

"That's fine." Sophie said. "Do you mind, Dad?" The look of worry was easing on her face.

"All right, but hands off my globe."

"Thanks," Sophie said to both of us. She revved the engine, and the car started down the road. Mike and I slowly made our way towards the bungalow. Halfway up the path, her car turned out of sight, and I decided dragging the frame was a better idea. Mike laughed.

"Don't worry, I won't tell Sophie." He took the frame out of my hand and carried it. I smirked at him; I had always liked Mike. Sophie was a wonderful kid, but she was far too serious. Mike gave her humour in her life, something she needed. As we neared my front door, Doris came out of her bungalow smiling widely.

"I'm so glad to see you're alright." She called hurrying towards us. "James told me what happened." I felt my face heat up with a blush.

"I'm fine, a lot of fuss over nothing." My chest felt tight and I couldn't look Doris in the face. Her son had killed my Molly. Did she know? Was she protecting him? I looked at her, she looked like she always did. Nothing in her face betrayed anything. Did she know her son was a murderer? Was that why she was nice to me? Did she know? Did she feel guilty? Did she think that Molly's death could be repaid with a few dinners and a token friendship? Or was she just as blind to her son as I had been? Was she taken in by his good boy act?

"Nothing stops this old bastard." Mike clapped me gently on the back, snapping me out of my spiralling thoughts.

"I'll let James know you got home safe; he was so worried about you." Doris said.

Was she warning him that I was on to him? Why else would she be so keen to let him know I was back?

"He's really taken a shine to you."

Was that a threat? Was she telling me that James knew that I knew and he'd be watching me?

"If you need anything don't hesitate to let me know."

"I'm fine, really. No need to fuss." I said a tad quickly as Doris went back inside.

Once inside, Mike set the frame down behind the door and stretched. I turned to the window, would Doris tell James I was home? Would he come tonight? No she'd tell him Mike was here and Mike was huge. James would stay away tonight at least.

"You ok there? You're sweating," Mike said.

"I'm fine." I wiped my brow. "Just tired." I looked around the bungalow for Molly, she wasn't there. "Sofa's not huge."

"I'm not huge, it's an optical illusion. Besides, it won't do me any harm for one night." He grinned at me. "I think that Doris lady has a soft spot for you. She was so relieved to see you home safe."

"Shut up." That would have made me laugh before. The idea that any woman would take an interest in me. But now it made my stomach roll. I had liked Doris, I'd eaten with her, had drinks with her, let my guard down. To know now that it was her son who'd killed my Molly. I couldn't bear it.

"Now!" Mike rubbed his hands together like an overgrown kid. "Let's order pizza."

One pizza and a violent, action-packed film later, Mike knocked back the last of my brandy and smiled at me.

"I'm glad you'll be staying with us," he said. I raised an eyebrow; the man had polished off a bottle that had been almost half full and had been getting progressively wobbly as the night went on.

"Yeah?"

"It'll be nice to have someone to have a drink with."

I nodded. I had forgotten Mike's dad had passed away only three years ago from cancer. Mike had been close to him from what Sophie said.

I reached over and patted his shoulder.

"Well, if you're looking for a drinking partner, then we will have to get you better at it, my boy," I said. "You're ten sheets to the wind and you've only had a few." Mike made a soft sound of agreement and yawned. "Well, I'm heading to bed. Come on, we'll get you a spare blanket." Mike followed me into the bedroom and took the blanket and a pillow. "You know where everything is if you need anything in the night."

"Yes, thank you." Mike wobbled a little when he turned around.

"He needs that frame more than I do," I muttered, heading in to turn the bed down.

Chapter Seven

I woke with a headache. Walking into the living room, I found the couch vacated and a note in the kitchen.

Art
Thanks for the couch.
Sorry to leave so early. I'm on the breakfast shift this morning.
I finish at 11am so will come around about 12, and pick you up. We can pick out some decorating bumph for the extension, help make it your own.
Remember to take your pills.
Mike

Glancing at the clock, I struggled to read it and frowned, not sure why something so familiar didn't make sense to me. I looked down at my digital watch, noting it was 9:30am. It was still early, that was good. I went to get a glass and had to pause for a moment, trying to remember which cupboard they were in. I had opened three different cupboards before I found them.

I grumbled while pouring myself a glass of water and drinking half of it. I set the half-full glass on the counter and dropped two dissolvable tablets into the water. It fizzed, and the cold water sat in my stomach like a lump of stone. "Stupid Mike and his drinking," I muttered. I downed the medicine before the fizz could stop. It hit my stomach hard, but when it didn't come back up immediately, I risked heading to the shower while I waited for Molly to appear. Keeping a hand on the wall, I shuffled down the short corridor to the bathroom and turned the shower on.

I stood under the spray a few moments later. Feeling my legs tremble, I sat down in the shower seat, turned the water temperature up, and closed my eyes while I waited for the pounding in my head to stop.

It didn't take long for the tablets to take the edge off the headache and the hot water to take the edge off my aching muscles. I stood slowly; the blood rushing out of my head; I wobbled as I turned off the shower but stayed on my feet.

"Careful, Art," Molly said. I jumped in fright. Most of the skin on her cheeks was gone now. Only fragments clung to bone. Her hair was all gone, showing where the skin had stretched and broken over her skull. I couldn't bear to see her like this. I had to do something and fast.

"You'll give me a heart attack popping up like that," I wrapped a towel around my hips.

"Sorry. You know when Sophie and Mike arrive in a little while, that will be it for me. You won't be able to help me."

"No. It'll be alright, I just need to think of something."

"They will take you to Sophie's house and you'll never get another chance." Tears fell down her face.

"Molly." I tried to reach out to her, but she took a step back.

"No, this is my last chance, you have to fix this now. Right now."

"But-"

"You were right, no one will listen, you have to get him yourself." Molly stood tall. "This man killed me, Art, you have to get him."

I nodded, the ice in my stomach spreading through my limbs. I walked into the bedroom, Molly on my heel.

I pulled on a pair of trousers and a shirt. I didn't look my usual debonair self, but at least I was decent. The panic cord in the bedroom was right by the bed and, reaching over, I pulled it.

"Give it a minute." Molly sat down on the bed next to me. I ignored the clicking sound her bones made as she did so. The smell that had been so overpowering was almost gone now. She no longer smelled of rot, instead she smelt like earth, dry and dusty. "They're on their way."

"Ok." My hands shook.

"You can do this, Art." She reached over and cupped my face in one of her hands. Her skin was cold and dry. I noticed one of her fingers was missing. She was falling apart in front of me.

"I can."

"My brave soldier," Molly's smile faded. "You believe me, don't you? That it was him that broke into our house one year ago." Molly looked away from me.

"I believe you."

"It was him. It was him who broke in here. It was him who hit you in the kitchen. He knows you suspect him. He was coming to do you in."

"Molly," I managed. My throat felt like a hand was around it.

"No Art." Molly looked at me, her milky eyes watery. "No Art, you're not seeing things, you're not paranoid, there is nothing wrong with your mind." She leant forward and wrapped her arms around me. "You're sharp as a tack." She sniffed. "You know the truth."

"I know."

"They've tried to make you confused, but it's all real. I'm real."

"I am confused." Molly held me tighter, her grip cold and hard.

"It's all those doctors," she whispered. "The children mean well sending you to them, but those doctors are just confusing you. You know what is real. You know that man was there the night I died."

"He was." Heat rushed to my face.

"The police know they made a mistake when I died. Everyone knows that there were two people in the cottage that night, but no one wants to admit that. They've tricked you so you don't embarrass them and show the world the police and the courts made a mistake. They've got the doctors to confuse you. It's all meant to confuse you, to stop you from going to the papers, to stop you from finding the warden."

"Yes." It made sense. Molly was right. I had never been one for hiding the truth. The warden was the one who had broken into the cottage, and it was him who had broken in here as well. He'd attacked me in my home. I was not losing my marbles. I was still sharp; I could still do the crossword in under ten minutes as long as it wasn't the Sunday edition. Someone with dementia couldn't still do that, could they?

"He's coming," Molly said. "The one who did it. He's coming to finish you off now. He knows you're weak." The door clicked open.

"Mr. Webb," the warden called. "Sir? Are you ok? It's James."

"I'm in here, lad." I reached over to the bedside table and took hold of my stick. "I've had a fall."

"He'll kill you if you let him." Molly glanced at the door, then back at me and back at the door again. "You've got to fight!" She stood up and put herself in the doorway. "I can't protect you." She was crying. "You've got to save me, but I don't want you to die."

"I won't." I gripped my stick hard, my grip as sure now as it ever was, and listened to the warden approach.

"Mr. Webb?" He stuck his head in through the door, forcing Molly away.

"Here, lad." I tightened my grip. "I fell in the shower; I think my ankle might be broken." I gestured with my free hand at my right ankle.

"I'll get an ambulance called and we'll get you sorted, don't worry."

"You can use my phone. It's over there." I pointed to the table beside the wardrobe. The warden nodded and turned his back to me.

Normally, I would never attack a man from behind; it's not the way to fight. But when you're at a severe disadvantage, and you have to win, sometimes you have to throw honour to the wind and use all your advantages. This warden saw me as a frail old man, an injured frail old man at that, and while he might be right, he didn't see me as a soldier who had survived two wars.

Ignoring the trembling weakness in my legs, I stood up tall. I raised my stick up high and brought it down with all my strength. It made a satisfying sound as it connected with the back of his head. The force of the blow rattled all the way up my arm, making me drop my only weapon. I cursed; it was on the floor, well out of my reach now. The warden staggered and fell forward, but he was still conscious. Turning, I reached over to the bedside table and grabbed my alarm clock. It was a solid old thing, just like me.

"You killed my wife," I told him.

"Wha…" he managed as blood ran from his head into his eyes. He went to wipe the blood away, and I lurched forward, the alarm clock held firm in my hand. I would not drop this one. I hit him across the face. His nose shifted unnaturally under the blow. The warden brought his arms up to shield his face. Pain spider-webbed across my fingers, and I almost lost my grip on the clock. I swapped hands.

"My Molly! She was my wife!"

The warden said nothing, only shouted noise at me.

"She was my wife!" I staggered forwards; I missed him this time as he stumbled backwards out of the bedroom into the hallway. "I'll kill you, you bastard."

"You need the walker," Molly said.

"It's in the living room." Pain lanced through my body. "I don't need the walker; I can get him." I hobbled forwards, ignoring the pain, all but forcing myself to breathe through it. The warden had fallen in the hallway and lay unmoving on the floor. I grinned. That bastard was mine. My legs all but crumpled under me when I reached him. I landed hard on my knees, still holding the alarm clock. I lifted it up and brought it down on him again, and again, and again. After the fourth strike, the blood on my hands made me drop the clock. My vision was black at the edges and my chest felt tight enough that I couldn't get a proper breath into my lungs, but I had done it.

I had saved Molly.

I fell backwards. I could feel the wiry carpet beneath me and the sticky warmth of the warden's blood. He had bled a lot; head wounds always did.

"Art, you did it." I could hear Molly speaking, but I couldn't see her. "You did it!"

"I saved you." I closed my eyes. "I finally saved you."

Epilogue

"I can't imagine it," the carer said as Sophie followed her into the dayroom. "He's such a gentle soul. I can't imagine him attacking someone like that without provocation."

"The old boy was a soldier; he knew how to hit him." Mike walked behind Sophie.

"Mike," Sophie admonished.

"Sorry love."

"I didn't mean to upset you," the carer said. "I just… I saw the newspaper yesterday, the court judgement, and I couldn't believe it."

"Damn paper," Sophie said. "Made Dad sound like a raving lunatic. He's never hurt anyone before."

"Or since," Mike said. "The judge knew that."

"He still ordered him to stay here, though."

"He did nearly kill that chap," Mike said.

"He's one of our most affable residents," the carer spoke up before Sophie could say anything else. "Although he has his moments. But the medication has prevented any more violent outbursts."

"That's good." Sophie hesitated a moment. "Honestly, do you think he's happy here?"

The carer smiled. "Yes, he is happy. But I don't think he always knows he's here."

"Well, that's something. He always hated hospitals."

"He's just over there, by the big window. Be patient with him. He's still not speaking." The carer gestured to the window, and Sophie glanced up. Seeing her father, she forced a smile and walked over.

"Hi, Art old boy," Mike said. "How are you?"

Arthur looked up.

"Hi Dad," Sophie knelt in front of the wheelchair and took her father's hand, he looked at her and frowned. "Do you know me?" Arthur went still and stared hard at her. "It's Sophie."

Her father continued to watch her for a long moment before looking away, out the window.

"He's not frightened, sweetheart." Mike gently squeezed Sophie's shoulder. As she stood, a shaking, aged hand reached out to find hers. She looked back, eyes wide, to see her father looking at her and smiling triumphantly.

"I did it." His voice was hoarse and weak. "I saved my Molly."

The End

About the Author

Katie Marie is a horror enthusiast and writer from Norfolk, England. She has been published in several anthologies and magazines, including The Horrorzines Book of Ghost Stories which won Best Anthology in the 23rd Annual Critters Readers' Poll.

Katie started writing while studying for her Law Degree at Aberystwyth University in the early 2000's and several years and stories later she received her Master's Degree and published her first novel.

You can connect with Katie on Facebook at katiemariewriter or on Twitter @KatieMarieWrite.

You can also visit her website, katiemariewriter.com to sign up for emails about new releases, short stories and blogs gushing about the horror genre.

Content Warnings

Dementia
Mental Illness
Death
Violence

More From Brigids Gate Press

Visit our website at www.brigidsgatepress.com

Coming September 2022

During the Spring Equinox underneath London, four people enter the caves, but only one will survive. Each trespasser must battle their own demons before facing the White Lady who rises each year to feed on human flesh.

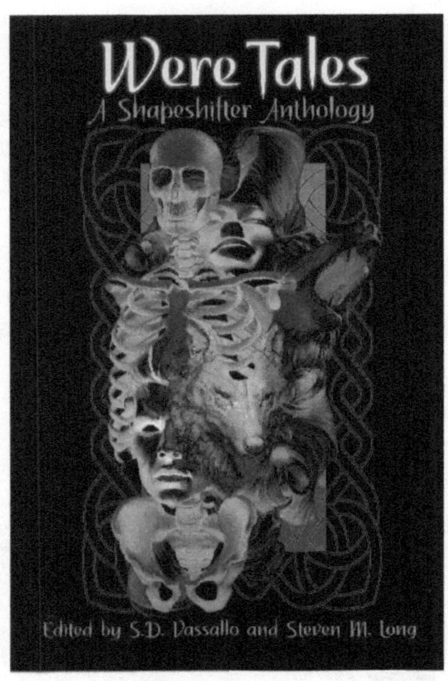

Published September 2021

Werewolves. Berserkers. Kitsune. From the most ancient times, tales have been told of people who transform into beasts. Sometimes they're friendly and helpful. Sometimes they're tricksters, playing jokes on their hapless victims. And sometimes, they're terrifying.

Were Tales is a collection of scary, thrilling, dark, mysterious, and even humorous short stories and poems of shapeshifters.

Published February 2022

A Quaint and Curious Volume of Gothic Tales; 23 stories of madness, pain, ghosts, curses, unspoken secrets, greed, murder, and one of the creepiest collections of dolls ever. Ranging from traditional gothic themes to more modern tropes, this anthology is sure to please the reader…and send a cold shiver or two down their spine.

So, come on in; enter the parlor, find a place by the fire, and experience the beautiful, dark, and occasionally heartbreaking stories told by the authors. The editor, Alex Woodroe, has passionately and carefully curated a powerful volume of stories, written by an amazing and diverse group of contemporary women writers.

Published April 2022

Sing O Muse, of the rage of Medusa, cursed by gods and feared by men…

From the mists of time, and ages past,
The muses have gathered; hear now their songs.

A web of revenge spun 'neath the moon,
A poet's wife who breaks her bonds,
A warrior woman on a quest of honor,
A painful lesson for a treacherous heart,
A goddess and a mortal, bound together by the travails of motherhood;
And more.

Listen to the muses, as they sing aloud…HER story.

Musings of the Muses, 65 stories and poems based on Greek myths, is an anthology of monsters, heroines, and goddesses, ranging from ancient Greece to modern day America. This anthology revisits those old tales and presents them anew, from her point of view.

Published May 2022

Welcome to the Weald.

The Five Turns of the Wheel has begun. With each Turn, blood will be spilled, and sacrifices will be made. Pacts will be made…and broken. Will you join the Dance?

In the Weald, the time has come for the Five Turns of the Wheel. Tommy, Betty and Fiddler, the sons of Hweol, Lord of Umbra, have arrived to oversee the sacred rituals…rituals brimming with sacrifice and dripping with blood.

Megan Wheelborn, daughter of Tommy, hatches a desperate plan to free the people of the Weald from the bloody and cruel grip of Umbra, and put an end to its murderous rituals. But success will require sacrifice and blood as well. Will Megan be able to pay the price?

Published May 2022

Decades after his grandfather was buried alive in a Californian gold mine, Dr. Nick Jones teams up with an adventure travel influencer to venture underground and film a documentary, telling the story of what really happened.

What should be a dream come true soon becomes a nightmare as someone or something stirs…BELOW.